*Echoes*

*In loving memory of*
*Georg & Gertrud Knabenbauer,*
*and of Kantimay Ghoshal.*

# *Echoes*

*by*

*Eva Maria Knabenbauer*

WINDHOUND PRESS

Copyright © Eva Maria Knabenbauer 2007
First published in 2007 by Windhound Press
24 St Clements Rd, Ruskington, Sleaford
Lincolnshire NG34 9AF

Distributed by Gazelle Book Services Limited
Hightown, White Cross Mills, South Rd, Lancaster, England LA1 4XS

The right of Eva Maria Knabenbauer to be identified as the author of the work has been asserted herein in accordance with the Copyright, Designs and Patents Act 1988.

All rights reserved. This book is sold subject to the condition that it shall not, by way of trade or otherwise, be lent, resold, hired out or otherwise circulated without the publisher's prior consent in any form of binding or cover other than that in which it is published and without a similar condition including this condition being imposed on the subsequent purchaser.

All of the characters in this book are fictitious and any resemblance to actual people, living or dead, is purely imaginary.

British Library Cataloguing in Publication Data
A catalogue record for this book is available from the British Library

ISBN 978-0-9542292-1-4

Typeset by Amolibros, Milverton, Somerset
This book production has been managed by Amolibros
Printed and bound by T J International, Padstow, Cornwall, UK

# Contents

| | | |
|---|---|---|
| Foreword | | vii |
| Acknowledgements | | viii |

## Bloc I

| | | |
|---|---|---|
| Frank | Room 137 | 3 |
| Joseph & Thekla | The Letter | 18 |
| Gerhard Fichte | The Chat-up | 32 |
| Erika | No Going Back | 41 |
| Willi | Ulterior Motives | 54 |

## Bloc II

| | | |
|---|---|---|
| Fräulein Vogel | Weathering the Storm | 73 |
| Brunhilde | Inheritance | 84 |
| Ina & Theo | Green-eyed Monster | 100 |
| Amadeus | Repercussions | 111 |
| Schulz | The Dear Boy | 125 |

## Bloc III

| | | |
|---|---|---|
| Bertrand | A Most Magnificent Peacock | 145 |
| Helga | Impressions | 161 |

# Foreword

The common thread running through all twelve stories of this collection is that they are based on subsidiary characters of my novel *Silent Shadows*. Mostly, the stories are snapshots of life in the former GDR or afford glimpses into the re-united Germany, and in this they are unashamedly political. But, above all, each story is about the trials and tribulations of the human condition, and I hope my readers will be as intrigued by the characters' challenges as I was in the writing of it.

Despite the characters' previous inclusion in my novel, each of their stories is well able to stand alone. Though I feel – and beg indulgence for saying so – having read *Silent Shadows* adds another dimension to the collection.

I have arranged the stories in such a way that the first five of Bloc I share being set in the pre Berlin Wall days of 1960 and 1961. The first story of Bloc II comes to an end in 1963, whilst the other four find their conclusions in post-1989 Germany. The two Bloc III stories take the reader to Kuala Lumpur and the Malay rainforest and to London.

# *Acknowledgements*

I am indebted to my fellow members of the Sleaford Writers Group, Lois Fenn, Malcolm Doughty, Dr Richard Shaw, Dennis Brett, Irene Rushton and Vernon Eric Bridges, for their comments and criticisms on the stories. I would also like to thank Jane F Tatam for editing and typesetting, as well as Eric Mahler for letting me display 'Promenadenring' on the cover.

*Bloc I*

# *Frank*

## *Room 137*

Having alighted from one of the wagons, young Frank hastened along the platform towards the head of the train. He stopped at the open door of the next, the third carriage. Right, he thought, steeling himself, that's it. From the corner of his eye he ascertained that a few steps behind him his superior, a higher-ranking border guard, was also approaching.

Giving an impression of nonchalance, Frank puffed up his cheeks before letting the air escape with a loud popping sound. He had been told that this idiosyncrasy of his made him look gormless. Annemarie had said so. But just now he had far more important worries: would his and Wilhelm's plan be successful? Wilhelm's fate hung in the balance, and his, Frank's, with it.

Before Sergeant Unrat could draw level, Frank rushed at the open wagon door. In his eagerness to get on board first, Frank elicited a curse when he knocked against Unrat's revolver – it was secured in its holster and tied to his belt.

Wilhelm was sitting on the left-hand side as he had said he would. Hunched over a magazine, his trademark blonde bob of hair partly hid his boyish face. Frank noticed with satisfaction that Wilhelm's stance appeared relaxed and that there were no telltale signs of fear.

When Wilhelm's corn-blue eyes briefly glanced up at him, giving a conspiratorial wink, Frank was instantly reminded of Annemarie, Wilhelm's sister. With eyes indistinguishable from those of her brother, she had last night flashed him a most promising look, which had managed to melt away his misgivings for the day to come.

At the end of today's shift he intended to meet her. She had initiated the date, and, assuming everything had gone well for Wilhelm, he, Frank, would be the harbinger of the good news. Maybe she would take him to her room? His eyes briefly glazed over at the thought of it. Until now, he had only glimpsed her 'boudoir' – the honey-coloured, frilly curtains had instigated this label. How heavenly to be alone with her! In anticipation of such delights he had brushed his teeth extra vigorously this morning, so much so that he had spat specks of blood into the wash basin. And because he had munched two crispy apples after lunch, his tongue still slid smoothly over their white enamel surfaces.

The gruff voice of his plump-faced colleague – because of his watery pale eyes and sparse sandy-coloured hair nicknamed 'Piggy-face' by some – shook Frank out of his deliberations: "Not so fast, young man. You'll do the geezers on the other side. I'll do this lot 'ere on the left." Showing off in front of the passengers, he boxed Frank in the ribs. "It looks the smaller pile, age before beauty, eh. Come on, hop it," he grunted when Frank, pretending not to have heard the command, stood his ground and proceeded to check the identity card of another passenger standing on the left-hand side.

'Piggy-face' snatched the pass from Frank's hand and pushed his young underling over to the right.

Frank's insides knitted into a tight ball and apprehension made him swallow hard. Sergeant Unrat had the reputation of being a stickler. What of the repercussions…?

Down the carriage, Wilhelm had witnessed the exchange. He looked thunderstruck and shot pleading looks into Frank's direction. Things were not going to plan. Wilhelm had counted on Frank checking him and everyone else in the left half.

The two young men had prided themselves on the thoroughness of their preparations. They felt sure that they had thought of all eventualities. But what they had not – could hardly have – foreseen was that today of all days Frank's usual colleague, who was easy-going and let Frank get on with the job, had for the first time ever reported sick. Sergeant Unrat, who had been about to go home at the end of his shift, was called back to cover the absence. None too pleased about his extended duties, he was not in a good mood and let his frustration out on Frank.

The young man stared at a white-faced passenger's identity card with unseeing eyes. Returning it to its owner, Frank noticed how, a couple of rows on, but out of his assigned area, Wilhelm's jaw had dropped and he was fidgeting. A quick glance over his shoulder confirmed to Frank that old 'Piggy-face' was being thorough since he carefully checked some passengers' identity cards against his listings of suspects. But then he would, wouldn't he!

What if our plan does go wrong? With the back of his

hand Frank wiped perspiration off his forehead, but the image of handcuffs would not be blotted out.

What if it should become apparent that he was ready to assist a so-called enemy of the people to escape? His father would never forgive him if ever he were to find out. "You should be grateful to live in the GDR's Workers' Republic," was one of his standard phrases when Frank moaned the slightest little bit about shortages. And if on such occasions his father was not rushed for time he would go on about the – in his view – exemplary Eastern health care, the provision of crèche facilities for working mothers, often conveniently at their workplace, as well as about the total non-existence of unemployment and prostitution. The latter topic was a particular hobbyhorse of his father's. "In our Republic no woman is forced for economic reasons to sell her body," he would boast. "Compare that with the state of affairs in the West where red-light districts abound and girls walk the streets to make money for their pimps." The word 'money', once uttered, would lead Frank's father on to hold forth about the Western capitalists who, never having been held responsible for their Nazi past, had grown rich on the backs of their fellow countrymen and women. According to Frank's father, in the East, the fascists had well and truly been rooted out.

Occasionally, in exasperation, Frank turned to his mother for support: "Father makes the place sound like paradise. He doesn't know how tired I am of his Party-talk and the speeches he makes me listen to. He goes well over the top. I mean, draping his Hero-Of-Work Medal right over your wedding photo!"

"Now, now," his mother would soothe him. "Don't forget Dad was always a staunch Union man all through the 'twenties and 'thirties. He never lost his idealism. Surely, your shared enthusiasm for motorbikes makes up for political differences?"

Somewhat placated, Frank could not but agree then. He loved to go riding with his father and to talk shop about bikes. That was when they were the best of friends.

Now, as Frank went about his business of checking passengers, and tried hard to push the worries about Wilhelm's undertaking to the back of his mind, another thought – it had to do with musical taste – gave Frank a stab. Father, he thought, would hit the roof if he knew about the Elvis Presley records, bought from undesirable characters, as his folks would say. Annemarie's house was the place he had to visit to listen to the music.

Frank looked at his watch. Not long and he would be with her. His heart was beginning to beat faster at the thought of it. For ages, well for at least three weeks, he had fantasised about making a move and to tell her how he felt about her.

If only Wilhelm will keep his cool! They might stand a chance after all.

Another glance over his shoulder told Frank that very soon now 'Piggy-face' would get to Wilhelm and check his papers.

Looking at another traveller's pass on his patch, Frank suddenly noticed, out of the corner of his eye, that Wilhelm had stood up from his seat and appeared to be heading for the exit.

The ensuing commotion erupted in front of Frank's eyes and ears as in a bad dream. He saw Wilhelm caught by the arm and pulled back to his seat by his hefty colleague who then rammed his knee against the young man's chest.

"Don't move!" the sergeant shouted, and he called to his young colleague, "Come 'ere, Frank! Quickly, man!"

Frank dropped his notebooks and rushed over to where Wilhelm was near to asphyxiation.

"Watch 'im," the sergeant growled and took out his revolver before removing his knee.

Sergeant Unrat thrust his hand inside Wilhelm's jacket and drew out a small bundle of papers. "These yours?" he asked.

Wilhelm nodded.

The sergeant studied the papers minutely. For long seconds he looked from Wilhelm to one of the documents. "That you?" he said, pointing to the photograph.

Wilhelm nodded again.

A heart-stopping few seconds later, in the dead silence which had descended over the carriage, Frank heard the sergeant say: "If that's you, I'm your twin brother," and he knew Wilhelm's fate was sealed. Maybe his own also?

"Come on, whose pass is it?" the sergeant sneered. He nudged Frank and grinned, and holding the photograph in front of his face, he asked, "What d'you think, Frank?"

Frank avoided looking at Wilhelm, mumbled something indistinct and shrugged his shoulders.

He felt desolate and ashamed and wanted to say: "If life is so brilliant here why keep people in as in a prison?" But of course he said nothing. Nobody else in the carriage said anything either.

In the past he had not really thought about the ones that got caught. They know the risk, he had told himself. But now with Wilhelm it was a different matter. Wilhelm was someone he liked and he was Annemarie's brother.

The nightmare situation continued with the sergeant pointing the revolver at Wilhelm. "Out!" he ordered, waving the weapon in the direction of the carriage door.

Once on the platform, he pushed Wilhelm, face

downwards, to the ground, the revolver aimed at the back of his head. He commanded Frank to signal to the driver to move the train out of the station. Frank then had to pull Wilhelm's arms behind his back, whence the sergeant kicked him in the face. As the train gathered speed, Unrat grabbed Wilhelm by the hair and made him watch as it disappeared from view.

Frank still said nothing.

Later, when Wilhelm had been taken away and Unrat boasted that because of his laudable co-operation Frank too would be entitled to special holiday bonuses, Frank felt sick to his stomach.

It took ages for Wilhelm to be driven away and for Sergeant Unrat to complete the paper work detailing the incident leading to Wilhelm's arrest. Apart from anything else, it meant that Frank had missed his precious date with Annemarie. They were to have met at Berlin Alexanderplatz – their most ambitious meeting place so far, as they usually met at Annemarie's house under the discreet eyes of her family.

Looking at his watch, Frank calculated – even after waiting for him, say for an hour – Annemarie should be back at home by now. So, he decided to go to her house.

But once he stood outside it, across the street, he hesitated. He gnawed his lip. How was he going to tell her and her parents about what he had witnessed? He wanted to minimise the family's upset, but realised that this was wishful thinking. What made the situation even harder was that the parents had been kept in the dark about Wilhelm's planned escape.

Anger welled up in Frank. Now that the initial trauma was subsiding, his critical capability returned. What had been done to Wilhelm was not right. Why shouldn't he be allowed to leave the country? (On a snooper's suspicion that he planned to do just that his friend's identity card had been taken away and, consequently, he had resorted to adapting a pass he had found on a bus.)

In the old days, Frank had not been interested in politics. He had not concerned himself with the official doctrine that escapees were Western spies intent on the destruction of the GDR. Like the rest of the jargon, it went in one ear and out of the other. But, much to his surprise, since mixing with Annemarie's folk, his attitude had changed and he had started to take an interest in the politics of the day. Having been present at some heated discussions, he too formed his own opinions. Unlike at home, the new people he mixed with were interested in his thoughts. At home with his parents the Party line was sacrosanct and different opinions were out of the question. For the first time in his life he was encouraged to think independently about issues, and he began to appreciate that matters were far from straightforwardly black and white.

Just as Frank had steeled himself for his sorry task, he saw a posh dark limousine draw up. Two plain-clothed men knocked at Annemarie's door and then entered the house. What did they want? It was not normal procedure to inform the relatives of an arrest.

Frank pictured them all, sitting in the living room, around the table behind Frau Hartung's piano. On hearing the news, he imagined her kind eyes filling with tears. But despite her distress she would retain her dignity. Her husband would most likely be pacing up and down like a caged lion. Annemarie's face, Frank thought, would wear an impenetrable expression. She would not say anything. No, not even under interrogation. But would she really hold out? He remembered overhearing a comrade in their canteen: "They all talk in the end."

He had asked him for an explanation and been told not to worry and to leave that aspect to the experts. "Your job is just to catch them."

Would Annemarie suspect him of treachery? He was the only outsider who knew of the plan. She knew his parents were Party members; nevertheless Annemarie had vouched for him.

He had met her at Wilhelm's twentieth birthday party. A friend of a friend had managed an invite for him. Pop music was currency and banned records were being exchanged. A new world had opened up.

As the time went by, Frank's anxiety increased. While the limousine stood solidly outside Annemarie's house, he could not make himself move from behind a group of nearby trees.

Sitting on the ground he must have dozed off, for the slamming of a door brought him to his senses. Flanked by the two men, Annemarie was being led down the steps. The handcuffs reflected the eerie light of the moon. As he watched her being bundled into the car, his heart reached out to her.

Trying to sort out his inner turmoil he roamed the quiet streets till early light.

"Congratulations," said Frank's father, looking up from his breakfast. His face was beaming. "I heard what happened," he explained. "Some of your work mates dropped by and told me about your heroics. They couldn't wait for you any longer and had to leave." Noticing his son's bemused expression, he asked, "You know what I think?" But without waiting for a reply, he went on: "That creep you helped to catch was most probably armed. Good job you acted quickly." He drained the last of his coffee. In his excitement, the liquid went down the wrong way and made him cough. Eventually, he said, "You know I'm really proud of you, didn't think you'd had it in you. I suppose you celebrated into the early hours?"

Frank did not answer.

"I thought I heard voices," his mother said, poking her head through the door."

"You heard me," said her husband. "Our Frank here has turned dumb. "Or maybe he's just modest?"

Frank did not know what to say. He managed an awkward smile before excusing himself from the room.

"No, wait! We understand. You're tired." His mother gave him a big smile. "Just one thing before you go. Earlier I had a message from your station. They are expecting you in Room 137 at three o'clock sharp, this afternoon."

Frank was stunned, but did not let it show. "Thanks," was all he said. His parents were not aware of it, but he knew what the room number signified. Sleep was now out of the question.

※

"Please, take a seat, Frank," said a friendly voice, and the well-dressed man it belonged to stood up from his leather chair. "I am Major Trapper, State Security," he said, and clicked his heels.

Having settled back behind his desk he immediately leaned forward and proffered a silver cigarette case.

"I don't smoke," Frank said. He was confused. The friendly reception was throwing him off course. He did not know what to expect; that, he thought, depended on whether

Wilhelm and or Annemarie had talked. Was he, Frank, to assume he was still in the clear?

"I have invited you for a little chat," the major said, after he had lit up. He smoked his cigarette in silence, all the while scrutinising the young man opposite him.

When the silence had become oppressive, he suddenly bent down, re-surfaced, and plonked a pile of records on the desk, right in front of Frank. They were Elvis Presley records.

"Do they look familiar?" the major asked sweetly. He patted the pile with his hand. Looking Frank in the eyes, he prompted: "Yes?"

The corner of Frank's mouth twitched and he sat up rigidly.

"Yes?" asked the major again. "Or is it, no? Say something!" He lifted several records from the top before letting them drop back onto the pile. "They should be familiar." His voice, which had been non-threatening then turned icy: "Because they *are* yours. Prohibited and yours!"

Frank could not think of anything to say. He just shook his head vigorously in response to the accusation and to gain more time. As soon as the records had landed in front of him on the desk, he thought that they were his.

Should he be relieved? This morning, when his mother passed on the message about the three o'clock appointment, he had wondered and feared whether a connection between him and the Hartungs had been established. The forbidden records had not featured. If the Stasi suspected him of aiding and abetting Wilhelm, it would make sense to pull him in for an official appointment. He did not think for one moment that they had called him to distribute laurels. His superiors could do that any time without special invitation.

What if the Stasi had nothing concrete on him? At least not yet. He might just have been seen in the company of Wilhelm or Annemarie. Someone might have reported him for entering their house? He just had to play it by ear.

Nevertheless, the Stasi had somehow got hold of his records! How? Wait a minute, he told himself. Are they my records? Is this Major Trapper only bluffing?

He decided, it was essential not to admit to anything. As far as his – and any other forbidden records were concerned – he and the Hartungs had always been so careful! After listening to them, they were hidden away in the loft.

"This is getting boring," Major Trapper hooted. He leaned back in his chair and once again smiled amicably: "I was hoping for a dialogue, and here I am listening to my own voice. Unless," he whispered ominously, "you're building up to tell me something, anything?"

Frank remained silent.

Suddenly, the major's fist came crashing down on the desk, making the pile of records slip. "I can do this another way! I am not wasting any more time." Leaning forward, he glared at the young man and told him point-blank that he had been found out.

Referring to the brother and sister Hartung as the 'subversive duo', he accused Frank of being in league with them.

Later, back outside in the street, Frank found it hard to recall exactly how the interview had progressed after the major's angry outburst. In the atmosphere of fear, the sequence of the arguments and the various accusations had become jumbled up in his mind. Even now he felt his sweat-soaked shirt clinging to his back.

He could no longer say whether it had been Wilhelm or Annemarie who supposedly had given him away as an accessory to the crime of Wilhelm's attempted escape from the GDR.

However, amongst his befuddled thoughts, one stood out crystal-clear: to redeem himself he would have to become an unofficial Stasi snooper. "It's up to you," the major had said. "Go to prison, or help us." With raised finger, he then went on to warn Frank that it was not enough just to agree to give information. "You'll actually have to come up with the goods."

Grinning all over his face, Major Trapper had finally stacked the Elvis Presley records into a neat pile before wrapping them in plain paper.

The records turned out to be his parting gift. "Enjoy them. Perks that go with the job." He seemed to be greatly amused and chuckled loudly.

Just before he had allowed Frank to leave, he slapped him playfully on the shoulder. "By the way," he said, "how very careless of you to write your name on one of the record sleeves. I expect you slipped up, just on the one, mind. All the other names had been erased. Last thing; don't forget your next meeting with me. Back here! In forty-eight hours sharp. Okay!"

"What a choice," Frank mumbled to himself, "prison or betrayal." Shaking his head, he walked on in a daze. Neither of the so-called options was feasible. He was not prepared to rot behind bars and he could not envisage treachery. What was he to do?

Twenty-four hours later Frank was back in Major Trapper's office. He made a sorry sight. His face covered in bruises, he sat slumped in the same chair he had sat in only yesterday. That was now a world away. Then, his future had still hung in the balance.

"What a stupid boy you are," he heard Trapper say. "By the way, your parents think so, too. Anyway, I gave you a chance, but you didn't take it. Why didn't you?"

Frank made no reply. After another sleepless night – he had been interrogated non-stop by different teams – he felt very tired.

When his chin touched his shirt collar, he partly opened his eyes. Below him, on the carpet, a pair of highly polished leather shoes entered his field of vision. He had not heard the major's approach but now felt his head being gently lifted up.

"Such a shame," the older man said, and he laid one hand on Frank's soft brown curls. "They will shave your head, you know." He started to run his fingers through the youngster's hair.

"Such a shame," he repeated, and his voice sounded consoling, but slightly breathless. "Maybe it's not too late? Do you understand what I am saying, Frank?" The major's cheek and mouth pushed so close that they obstructed Frank's vision. "What do you say, sweet? It's in my power to solve your predicament. All you need to do is to be nice to me. Your attempted escape, well, that was a misunderstanding, wasn't it? You were on the way to an assignment in the West, weren't you?"

"I bloody well was not, you filthy pervert!" Summing up all the force he was capable of, Frank pushed Trapper away. He had listened to the man with mounting suspicion, thinking at first that surely it could not be. But now there was no longer any doubt in his mind as to the other's intention. "You make me sick!" he shouted.

"You'll live to regret this," the major said coldly, returning to his chair behind the desk. "The next couple of years will be no picnic for you. I had my doubts about you, so I put you under strict surveillance, and, sure enough, you fell into the trap." He started to giggle hysterically. "Into the trap set by Trapper, do you see?"

Frank wanted nothing more to do with the man. He stood up, turned his chair around, and sat down facing the wall.

When the two police officers the major had requested earlier came into the room, he became business-like and off-hand. "Take him away," he said, with a dismissive gesture towards Frank.

# Joseph & Thekla

## The Letter

In the late afternoon sunshine, a tall sinewy figure moved unhurriedly along the glistening dirt track, which a hundred yards further on would turn into a proper suburban street with elevated pavements, street lamps and even lollipop trees. He was Joseph Kowalski. Carrying two sacks of goat fodder in one hand and holding a basket with newly dug potatoes in the other, he stopped outside the gate of a kind of afterthought-dwelling, seemingly erected once the street with its lines of two-storey houses had already been completed.

Old Joseph pushed the dangling garden gate fully open, and having gone through without setting any of his load down, he kicked with the underside of one of his clogs against the horizontal bar at the bottom of the gate. Giving a judder it neatly clicked shut.

Joseph straightened up, enjoying the warm sun on his

back. The whole day had been glorious, right from early morning. A summer's day in a hundred, he thought, and as an additional bonus, his visiting granddaughter, Anni, would be greeting him any minute. He felt blissfully happy, without a care in the world.

Appreciating the abundance of the blooms around him, he breathed in their scent deeply as he started to walk along the slabbed path to his and his wife's little home. It looked pretty with its two colourful window boxes at the front and the freshly painted woodwork.

As he often did, he stopped halfway along the path to take proprietary pleasure in the view. He liked to look at the dwelling from some distance away as he knew that on closer inspection the lack of care in the construction would make him groan – even though he had done his best in dummying up the sloping brickwork, and he had filled in many gaping holes.

Wearing his old but comfortable clogs on large, bare feet, he leant the sacks with fodder against the side wall, and noisily climbed the two cement steps before entering the tiny hall of what was in effect a glorified large shed. The entrance door was as always in the summery weather wide open and once inside the hall he kicked off the clogs and shoved them out of the way against the skirting.

Barefoot he continued into the kitchen-come-eating area and on into the single bedroom and partitioned-off box room. "Frau! Anni!" he called for his wife and granddaughter – rather pointlessly, it has to be said, as neither of them could possibly escape his searching gaze if they were anywhere in the whitewashed, minimally furnished rooms.

He gave a small squawk of disappointment and put the basketful of earth-caked potatoes down onto the scrubbed kitchen table. Two pine benches, shelves full of crockery, a worktable with drawer next to the black stove completed the inventory.

Opa, as everyone called Joseph, went over to the cooking range. Lifting the lid off the one parked pot, he saw that tonight's dinner would be fruit soup with dumplings. He gave the dark red gelatinous stuff a stir and hooked out one of the juicy plums, followed by a mouthful of sweet floury dumpling. The soup had been cooling for some time and was lukewarm; it would taste even better once cold. His wife, Thekla, must have finished with the cooking a while ago; and as if in confirmation, he touched the surface of the stove; it was quite cold.

On his way out through the hall, Opa risked a quick glance into the walk-in larder. "Hmm," he murmured, and widening his nostrils he drew in the fresh crusty bread aroma. The round-shaped loaf lay, at nose level, partially wrapped in a tea towel on the breadboard. But he resisted the temptation, shut the door and slipped back into his clogs. The wooden floorboards gave one more pained squeak and he was back outside in the garden.

"Frau! Anni!" Joseph called again, as he encircled the garden home. But still he got no answer.

A bird's cry overhead made him look up at the nominally elevated roof and, with a heavy sigh, he noticed a loose strip of felt.

The place was meant to have been only temporary. His wife Thekla, Oma, and he had moved into it some time after their flat had been reduced to rubble at the end of the war. But, on the plus side, the makeshift accommodation was surrounded by an acre of land, which they had transformed into a sizeable vegetable plot and a small flower garden. It had made them self-sufficient and they had not applied to be re-housed. On the contrary, they had kept a low profile in the hope that the authorities would forget about them.

It was only after Granddad Joseph had reached the chicken coop and the stable for the she-goat he finally saw a sign of human life. He glimpsed Thekla in the process of opening the door of the nearby toilet hut, ready to step down.

"That bucket needs emptying," she said – catching him look at her – but staying put until he came nearer. Holding her nose, she lifted the round cover before lowering it back over the hole in the bench. "Anni might not mind the stench. But I certainly do."

"Isn't she back then?" Joseph frowned. All at once he felt coldness breathing down his neck. "She should be here," he said insistently, and fidgeted with his braces.

When his hard leathery hands rubbed several times over his shiny bald, rosy pate, his wife cringed at the sound. "How often do I have to tell you, that sandpaper noise you make gives me the goose pimples. And don't rub your foot over the earth either."

Not expecting an answer, Thekla took a couple of steps in the direction of the railway line, which ran along the bottom of the vegetable patch. "Anni must have missed her train." Still looking in direction of the rails, Thekla thought aloud, "The next one won't be for another hour and a half, so that will be the earliest she can be at the station." Turning around to face Joseph, she added soothingly, "Don't let's worry."

But despite the displayed confidence, Thekla, too, was anxious.

Well, she did not quite know what to think. Gazing towards the rails again, a multitude of thoughts crossed her mind.

The normally easy-going Anni had seemed preoccupied; references to the future had evoked indistinct mutterings and little else by way of an answer. What she took to be her granddaughter's evasions had made Thekla wonder. Was Anni planning the unmentionable, was she about to run into a fellow's arms? She wouldn't leave her parents, would she?

Unless… . Thekla blushed, remembering her one act of rebellion when she had been Anni's age. Could history repeat itself?

Against her parents' wishes, Thekla had gone out with Joseph, who was not considered an eligible future husband. Everybody in the small village near the Polish border praised Joseph for being hard-working and kind, but he was a landless farm worker and his aspiration to train as a country vet was laughed at.

Thekla, so it was decided, would marry a rich farmer's son.

In her desperation, the twenty-year-old confided in and was given support by her maternal grandmother, and with her financial help Joseph qualified and set up practice further West in Rathenow.

Now, Anni, so Thekla reasoned with herself, knew about her grandparents' struggles to be together – she, Thekla, had spoken of it often enough, all the while stressing to her granddaughter that should the need arise not to hesitate and to talk any personal problem over with her. Therefore, Thekla thought, Anni would have said something, surely, and Thekla, having talked herself into a positive stance, felt reassured that Anni would be on the next train. After all, Anni was very close to her, just as close as she, Thekla, had been to her own grandmother.

The trouble was, Thekla's tender hope soon crumbled.

What if Anni's supposed difficulty was nothing like the one she, Thekla, had experienced? Would Anni still have wanted to confide to her grandmother then?

It seemed that Thekla was back to her starting point: would Anni be returning tonight? Yes, or no? Her heart sank. To make matters worse, an inner voice reprimanded her for having jumped to the conclusion that Anni was head over heels in love.

The longer Thekla ruminated, the more convinced she became that Anni was not about to elope in order to be with a boyfriend or lover. No, it did not feel like it. For one thing, there would have to have been some sort of contact, and there had been none. Anni had been with her or with Joseph all the time and she had not spoken to any stranger before going on her Sanssouci day trip.

It flashed through Thekla's mind, if Anni was running anywhere, she was more likely to be running from rather than running to.... Thekla knew that Anni hated the GDR, and she had been prevented from studying because of her political views.

Behind her, Thekla heard Joseph cough. To make his presence felt, she thought. How long had she been standing separate from him, lost in her thoughts?

Feeling his gaze on her back, she again turned around, and, remembering him telling her that today's young girls were as politically engaged as the menfolk, she drew a heavy breath. She could not deny, girls too were seeking their fortune across the border all the time. How the times had changed. In her young days girls knew better than to plunge into politics.

Joseph who had felt inordinately happy all day was loath

to give in to feelings of foreboding and clung on to his wife's explanation of the missed train.

"I did as you asked and had a good look around," he said, jauntily, as Thekla was about to go past him. And he started to talk to her about the state of affairs on the allotment, where he had just come from.

At one point, he lifted his hand up to his pate again, but he held back from stroking there.

"I'm afraid," he said, summing up, "the weeds are taking over, especially up on the steep hill." He gestured to knee height. "We've got to clear them, and do it soon. By the way," he added, smiling, "I've brought some of your favourite salad potatoes. They are on the kitchen table."

A fond expression in his eyes, Joseph looked at his wife of fifty-five years. Thekla barely reached to his shoulders. She was wearing one of her usual brown, slightly flared, woollen skirts, held up with an elastic waistband. And as she chuckled at their fluffy white kitten, which had started rolling about at her feet, her dome-like protruding tummy appeared to be jumping up and down under the cloth. It made him think about the ravages of time on her figure – and on his as well – but he knew that on the inside she – and he – had not changed at all.

Picturing young Thekla, his eyes were beginning to glaze over. A nudge of his wife brought him back down to earth.

"Did you know you've torn your shirt?" she said. "The barbed wire, I suppose. Anyway, you better take it off so I can mend it."

Without a word, he unbuttoned his shirt and handed it to her, and for the moment he had forgotten about Anni's lateness; everything seemed well again with the world. Thekla was her normal tranquil self – or so he thought.

As she turned to go indoors, he said, "I'll start the watering after I've had a smoke."

He walked past the chickens in their enclosure, and then past the underground cellar he had built six years ago. Steps led down into the caved-out chamber, five by four metres in size. He had needed to brick up the walls and fix a ceiling made of boards to stop the constant trickle of sand. It had been an arduous task but well worth the effort. For they could now store manifold items in the stopgap cool room: Thekla's preserves, barrels with fermenting Sauerkraut, pickled gherkins, salt meat, as well as their fresh goat's milk, to name a few.

At the woodshed Joseph sat down in a wicker chair with bulging stuffing and filled his pipe with home-grown tobacco. He was proud of last year's harvest. The leaves, the size of his hand, had been strung up on lines as if they were washing hung out to dry.

Smoking his pipe counted as one of his favourite leisure activities. But just now, sitting out here in front of his shed, away from Thekla's comforting company, he grew anxious again. Why was Anni late? She was usually very reliable. What if something had happened to her? While she was under his and Thekla's roof, they were responsible for her.

To his disdain, he remembered feeling uneasy about the way Anni had said goodbye to him in the morning. He thought she had been unaccountably intense. But why should that have been so? She had only gone on an excursion to Sanssouci! Why had she covered him with kisses and clung on to him as if she was never going to see him again?

Come on, enough of this hysteria, he scolded himself. And to dissipate his sombre mood, he thought of the game of chess after dinner, which they had promised each other. It was the anticipation of measuring himself against a youthful opponent that cheered him up, as well as the hard labour of pumping cans full of water from the underground well.

Shortly after seven o'clock Thekla returned. She touched Joseph on the arm and motioned to the bottom of the garden. "Let's go and wave to Anni," she said.

But however carefully they checked the windows of the passing train, they could not detect their granddaughter on board. Surely Anni would have expected her grandparents to look out for her and be at a window! Especially since she was late. At any rate, at the sight of Thekla or Joseph, or both of them in the garden, it was the accepted practice for family to wave.

"We won't know for sure for the next half hour, maybe even for longer if Anni dawdles on the way from the station," Thekla said after a while, though she did not sound convincing. "Come and have something to eat. Anni's portion will keep."

Thekla avoided looking at her husband, and Joseph too stared in front of himself. Separately, each was filled with foreboding. But as they walked side by side to their bungalow, neither of them voiced their worries. It was as if both of them were afraid to talk of the devil and make him appear.

Passing the letterbox, Thekla noticed the daily newspaper sticking out of it, and she retrieved it.

Joseph fiddled absentmindedly with the paper whilst listlessly eating his evening meal. Once more, a juicy plum on his spoon was allowed to slip back into the syrupy soup. It landed standing proud. He looked at it with distaste, before pushing the still half-full plate aside. "I can't…" he said.

He picked up the paper, ignored the front page and turned directly to the middle pages. An envelope in Anni's hand, addressed to Oma and Opa Kowalski slipped onto the table. "God, no," was all he said, having grown pale. Without a postage stamp affixed to the envelope, Anni had to have left it this morning before going on to Potsdam.

He held the letter in his left hand and knew... . Without reading it, he knew that Anni would not be back, not later this evening, not ever. Looking at Thekla, but not seeing her, he allowed the envelope to fall back onto the smooth table-top.

With a tired movement, he lifted his right hand, opened its palm, and gazing blankly into the flat of it, he kept shaking his head. He felt bereft. He had a sense of colour having gone from his life, leaving bleakness behind. When shutting his eyes, he thought he heard the flutter of unseen humming birds' wings, until the sound died.

Eventually, he again said, "I can't... . You read it, please," and he pushed Anni's letter across the table towards Thekla.

Hesitating, Grandma Thekla picked it up. Having extracted the one sheet of paper from the envelope, she unfolded it and did as asked.

"Dear Oma! Dear Opa!"

Seeing that the written text was only short, she scanned ahead. What she read confirmed her fears.

Despite her sorrow, she sensed that Joseph would be the one harder hit. There was nothing she could do to change that.

*"By the time you read this,"* Thekla almost whispered Anni's words, but read them out from beginning to end, without stopping, *"I should be safely in the*

West. I am sorry to have to spring this news on you like this.

"I thought of talking to you about my decision to leave but it would not have been fair to you. Nothing you could have said would have changed my mind. Also, I didn't want you to get involved in this. Should things not go according to plan you can't be held responsible. I will write to confirm my safe crossing as soon as possible. I will also let Mum and Dad know.

"Please do not worry about me. I have thought long and hard about my future – I have none here. Thank you for everything you have done, and most of all, thank you for being there for me.

"With all my love,

"Anni"

Noticing the PS, Thekla continued reading: "Maybe we will meet again, sooner than we can presently hope. After all, The Thousand-Year-Reich only lasted twelve. So, who can say?"

Thekla looked up at Joseph. He sat all crumpled up in front of her and her heart went out to him. It struck her there and then that he hurt the way she would do should she never be in the position to see little six-year-old Hans again. She was upset about Anni, there was no doubt about it, but Anni was capable. Barring bad luck and misfortune, she was bound to make a success of her life in the West. Little disabled Hans, however – well, he needed his old grandma. His mother could not manage him on her own. He was a major reason Thekla had to go on living – apart from being there for Joseph of course. She did not need confirmation, she just knew that his affection for Anni, though different, was nevertheless comparable to her own love for little Hans. His mother, Leni, Thekla's youngest daughter, brought him over, once every fortnight and he stayed on for a couple of days and nights. While with his grandparents, Leni got a break from caring for her son. Her husband had found the boy too much of a burden and left.

Little Hans, Hänschen, Thekla called him, was mentally retarded. Not able to speak properly and walking with callipers, he nevertheless expressed his happiness to see her by smacking wet kisses all over her face. He understood all right…

The two old people sat for ages facing each other across the table, assimilating the shocking news. The light dimmed and still they sat, hunched over on their chairs, the plates uncleared in front of them.

When they finally talked, their voices scratchy like rusty hinges, they discussed, at some length, the implications for Anni and for the rest of the family. They ascertained what they had to do.

First and foremost, they concluded, Anni's parents had to be told. But how were they to go about this?

Joseph and Thekla had no telephone. But one of them could go to the post office early tomorrow morning and book a call to their daughter in Aschersleben.

However, they soon dismissed that idea – no private conversation would be possible as the call was bound to be monitored by the State authorities. Writing a telegram or a letter posed the same problems of surveillance, and in the case of a letter it would take too long to get there.

"I'll go myself," Joseph said at last. "Yes, first thing in the morning I'll be on the train. Better that they hear it from me."

※

Joseph spent a near sleepless night. Next to him, Thekla was also tossing and turning. They were both going on eighty. How long had they got at that age? Was it likely that they would see Anni again? And what would happen to her, should she get caught?

Amongst Joseph's thirteen grandchildren Anni was special. She was interested in his experiences from the past. She did not flick her head upwards to the ceiling, let alone droop her jaw or make that particular circular movement with her hand as if she were playing a music box as soon as he talked of hardships. With her he could relax, sit in silence without feeling uncomfortable.

As the years rolled by in front of his eyes, he saw her grow up into a young lady. His eyes moistened and welled over as he remembered.

Only this morning she had been walking about the place before leaving for Sanssouci – well, that was where she said she was going. Now that things had fallen into place, he understood why she had whizzed about looking at this, touching that.

He had heard her in the stable talking to the goat and imagined that she had buried her face in the animal's fleece. He had even seen her climb up into the hayloft.

He remembered times further back: saw her playing in the sandpit with bucket and spade. Many a time she had tried to build a pond to sail her toy clipper; she had even lined the hole in the ground with cardboard and sacking. But each time she filled her pond up with water, to her dismay, the water kept soaking away. He had comforted her and explained…and filled up an old bathtub for her.

When she was a little older he had taken her fishing in a boat on the River Havel. She had never complained of being bored.

She had accompanied him to the wood where they collected fallen branches from the forest floor for the cooking and heating. She had helped with the sawing. Would she remember any of this?

In retrospect he wished he had talked with her about the East German situation. He knew she felt strongly about it, but true to form he always changed the subject, saying that he had never allowed politics into the home or his three sons would have come to grief. (They had been left and right wing supporters in the 'thirties.)

As Joseph lay there pondering the past, a last remark of Anni's came suddenly to his mind. He had thought that she had made it to ease the goodbyes. "Something I've wanted to ask you for years," she said, smiling, "why is it that the sides of your nostrils always turn white when you are angry? As a little girl I used to avoid you when I noticed it."

Joseph had been lost for an answer. And now as he pictured his granddaughter asking her question, his chest heaved with suppressed sobs.

But by the time light sneaked in from behind the curtains, he had grown calmer. I mustn't feel sorry for myself, he thought. This is not about me. She needed to break free and I have to respect that. She hasn't died, remember!

# Gerhard Fichte

## The Chat-up

God, it was hot today! Beach weather. Instead, here he was hanging about on a sweltering station platform in Brandenburg, surrounded by noisy fellow conscripts.

As an image of golden sand and smooth glinting sea flashed before Gerhard's eyes he longed to be at the Baltic coast. Just now, his parents and younger brother were on holiday there. They were sure to be enjoying themselves.

Gerhard stuck a finger between neck and collar of his cumbersome uniform, trying to widen the gap. But he didn't have much success.

He sighed. For the first time his family had gone camping to the seaside without him. If it were not for his recent call-up he too would be lying in the sand dunes, camouflaged in his favourite hollow in the shade of pine trees.

Gerhard took a handkerchief out of his breast pocket and dabbed his forehead. He looked around. He felt bored and it didn't help that he thought it would be ages before they were given their orders.

On the other side of the platform a number of passengers were heading towards a waiting train. As he idly watched, Gerhard's attention was drawn to a girl or young woman. Unlike others aiming to board the waiting train, she was not carrying a heavy suitcase. All she had with her was a bag and she was striding along easily. Dressed in a floral summer skirt – it whipped wagtail-like with every step – she wore a tight-fitting white blouse. Shamefacedly, he imagined her in a skimpy bikini.

As she walked closer, Gerhard thought that there was something familiar about her. Where had he seen her…?

Yes, of course… . He had suddenly twigged. She was Anni, his former classmate. She and her friend, Karin, had sat steps away from him.

But how could it be that she was here? According to rumours he had heard she'd left for the West. He looked again, to make double-sure. Definitely, it was Anni. But what was she doing here? Gerhard's curiosity was inflamed.

During their last year at school together, he had tried to 'go steady' with her – in retrospect, he had to smile at the phrase. But he had not been able to emulate those of his chums who had regular girl friends.

As the distance between Anni and him diminished, he remembered how, summoning up his courage, he had asked her out to the cinema. Only to be rebuffed. "Haven't got the time, sorry. Too much to do," had been her laconic reply. But the smile accompanying her refusal had kept his hope alive. Indeed, on the occasion of the annual dance school ball, held to show off everyone's acquired proficiency in ballroom dancing, he had been her main dancing partner. And at the end of the evening he had accompanied her home. Before she disappeared indoors, he had given her a chaste kiss.

Gerhard watched as Anni came closer still. To get on to the waiting train, she would have to pass him, and his fellow conscripts. But she was not looking his way. Probably intentionally, he thought, to avoid eye contact with anyone from his group. The unsupervised young men were a rowdy lot.

Drawing level with Gerhard, Anni continued to look straight ahead and walked by.

He was disappointed that she had not seen him. But he wasn't going to let the chance to talk to her slip through his fingers. So he followed her, and a few steps away from the others, he called out her name – not too loudly, so as not to draw the group's attention.

What happened next he thought mighty odd. Why in heaven's name did she not turn around? Granted, just for a moment, she had hesitated, but then she carried on walking as if he didn't exist.

Gerhard couldn't make it out. She had to have heard him. He had spoken clearly enough. He had expected her head to spin around. Surely, anyone hearing him – or herself – being addressed on unfamiliar ground in the middle of nowhere would turn to look?

That she was Anni Gerhard was more convinced than ever. After all, she had passed him at very close quarters.

What he didn't appreciate at the time was that unwittingly he had placed her in an impossible situation. Only later did her odd behaviour make sense.

As far as Anni was concerned, it was essential that nobody should recognise her. The overriding thought in her mind was that she must not be found on GDR soil – not after her staged escape over a week ago.

Consequently, hearing herself called by name, she was scared out of her wits and all she could think of doing was to pretend ignorance and walk on as quickly as possible. (Actually – though unnoticed by Gerhard – she had shot a sidelong glance in the direction of the speaker and realised he was Gerhard. Not daring to look properly she had swiped at an imaginary wasp to get a quick peek.)

Anyway, to Anni's even greater horror, her former school pal was not prepared to let the matter rest. He followed her and tapped her on the shoulder.

"What are you doing here?" he said. "I heard you'd left."

"Who do you think you are talking to?" Conjuring up a disdainful hand gesture, she somehow managed to sound offhand and angry.

"Anni," he said.

"I'm not Anni!" Facing him fully, she thought, *you idiot! Why don't you leave me alone? Don't you understand anything?*

Her outright denial had taken his breath away. He kept shaking his head in disbelief. "Don't give me that," he said hoarsely. He cleared his throat. "You must be Anni. Stop play-acting." His eyes pleaded with her.

Anni couldn't give the game away. She had notified her family of her escape from East Germany, and she knew that giving the news to her parents was tantamount to informing the authorities. In defiance of them, under the cloak of darkness, she had returned to be with Rudolf, to spend precious time with him. Now that she was escaping for real, she could not be found out. Why wouldn't Gerhard shut up? Didn't he realise the danger he was exposing her to? He couldn't be that thick, surely? Her message was clear enough. She'd always thought he liked her.

There was desperation and raw anger in her voice as she shouted at him: "Leave me alone and stop pestering me!"

At that, the other recruits were beginning to take an interest. They approached, jeering and whistling.

Anni knew she had to do something. She couldn't wait for the others to become suspicious. What if they twigged? Earlier on, Gerhard had referred to the rumour that she'd left. What if he let on about that to them?

So, feeling petrified, but with genuine rancour in her eyes, she simply turned on her heels and left Gerhard standing on the platform, oozing incomprehension.

And while she rushed to her train, she could hear Gerhard's querulous voice trying to convince his jeering and whistling comrades that they had not witnessed a chat-up that had gone wrong. "I just wanted to say hello, that's all," he insisted, and he doggedly repeated that he had been in the same class as her at school.

Before long the rest of the group lost interest in Gerhard's supposed escapade. They grumbled about being stranded in Brandenburg and wondered about the orders they were about to receive.

In the meantime, Anni's train was still standing on the platform. The writing on the board told Gerhard that there were a few minutes yet until departure. The destination was Potsdam. What business had she there, he asked himself? Maybe she was on her way to Berlin?

Berlin! He stood up straight. That's where two million Easterners had crossed the border into the West – supposedly she had even been one of them.

And then, as Gerhard kept staring at the furthest carriage, the one Anni had got into, he suddenly knew…

All at once the denial of her identity made sense. She had rushed away from him because she couldn't risk questions to do with that rumoured escape. Of course, she couldn't. Not if she was about to make the gossip come true!

Gerhard was now convinced of Anni's plan to defect. She was on her way out all right. As for the rumour he had heard, well, that seemed to be at odds with what was happening in front of his eyes. Okay, so he could not work out how the tale had come about. Never mind. There was bound to be an explanation. But right now, it wasn't something he chose to concern himself with.

As Gerhard continued to ponder the situation he felt, all of a sudden, unnerved. For the first time in his life he was faced with a thorny dilemma. What was he going to do about Anni's plan? It was decision time.

His duty as an upright citizen, as a member of the FDJ Youth Movement, as a soldier, dictated that he haul her from the train to prevent what he saw as her impending illegal escape. He looked at the station clock. There would be enough time for him to get to the carriage and stop her.

So, why wasn't he on his way there?

If only she had been someone else… . There would be fear in her eyes. She might cry, fight even. Would he need to use force? His legs seemed strangely weak. He stood immobile as if nailed to the ground.

Bourgeois sentiments! Pull yourself together, he reprimanded himself. She's an 'enemy of the people'. That's what counts.

"Enemy of the people," he mouthed, hoping to give himself courage. But he was still inert, standing on the same spot as before.

Enemy of the people, he repeated, soundless this time. It was a phrase he had been bombarded with, at school, in his army training. It was in heavy print in the newspapers, plastered on billboards. A well-oiled slogan indeed. He himself had used it. But what did it actually mean? He thought he knew...

From the recesses of his mind certain memories crystallised: another fellow pupil, Sybille, had spoken the very phrase in class, during that fateful German lesson...Parmenides had been teaching them...

They had been reading Anna Seghers' *Das Siebte Kreuz* in class. One of the characters in the book, a young boy, had his bike stolen. The Gestapo got involved. They suspected that an escaped prisoner from a concentration camp had taken it and they wanted a detailed description of it. The boy had scraped every penny together to buy his most treasured possession, but his memory suddenly became rather vague as he realised that the price of its return would be the recapture of the prisoner. He didn't want that.

Everyone in class, including Anni, agreed that the boy had done the right thing and Parmenides moved on to another topic. That was when she had put up her hand. "Would you praise me if I were to help a Stasi prisoner to escape?" Anni said.

Gerhard remembered that a hush fell over the class. Parmenides screwed up his eyes and mumbled ineffectually. (The lack of tongue-lashing was to cost the teacher dear. He was moved in disgrace to a crummy village school where, finally, he retired.)

But Sybille, who had jumped to her feet, took charge. "What a stupid question," she proclaimed. "Any prisoner of the Stasi is an enemy of the people. Everybody knows that." Self-satisfied, and nodding her head, she had sat down again. There you have it, said her demeanour, and she started scribbling in her notebook.

For a brief moment Gerhard wondered if Sybille had retained her old certainties. About six months ago he had seen her working in a mundane hairdressing salon. Should he read anything into it? Be that as it may, it didn't help him with the problem at hand.

As he kept standing on the station platform, trying to make up his mind what to do about Anni, he was distracted; thoughts and images concerning the escaped prisoner kept assailing him. What if the boy in the story had been true to the then Party-dictates? Surely, he would have been racked with guilt…

Supposing if, Gerhard asked himself, the present government turns out to be sullied, would he not make himself an accessory for unthinkingly doing the Stasi's bidding? The defence of 'Following Orders' would not save him from responsibility. Supporters of the Third Reich had learned this to their cost.

Once more, Gerhard dabbed his forehead with his handkerchief. The trouble was, he didn't actually believe it was Western propaganda that thousands of people were said to escape every week. Amongst their number were many from his own hometown. He knew for a fact some at least weren't enemies of the State… . His head was aching from the dispute going on inside. But he had a duty to think. That was after all the point of his schooling, wasn't it? Why hadn't he debated the official views before, looked at them properly for himself? It was thanks to Anni…

A swishing sound alerted him to the fact that the Potsdam train was moving out of the station. A sigh of relief slipped from his lips. Too late to do anything now, he thought. Thank God.

The train accelerated. It disappeared into the distance. But Gerhard kept looking. What a ridiculous idea, he thought, Anni an enemy... . She was voting with her feet...

Gerhard breathed in deep. He stretched to full height. He felt grown up. Good luck, Anni, he thought.

As for himself, he had no intention of following her example. To be content, he had to be in sight of Aschersleben's five-hundred-year-old church tower and to hear the bells. Bad enough to be temporarily away...

"You can't win them all," said a voice behind him.

Turning around, Gerhard grasped that his fellow conscript, Walter, was referring to the supposed unsuccessful chat-up.

Gerhard smiled. "How right you are. She won."

# *Erika*

## *No Going Back*

Erika had been soaking herself in the newly installed bathtub for several minutes; its avocado colour was the envy of her friends. In East Germany in the fraught days of 1960, a coloured suite, undamaged, was a luxury. As she lay relaxing in the hot foam, resting her head against a pink rubber cushion attached to the gleaming surface opposite the gilded taps, she fancied being a courtesan from history, preparing for an assignation. She raised a well-formed frothy arm out of the water as in an imperial greeting and imagined that from above and around her the cream-coloured ceramic tiles dripped their approval.

Holding on to the side of the tub, she pulled herself up, and, reaching for the tablet of sweet-scented soap, she started to lather her left knee and thigh before moving up to her right shoulder.

"No system as usual," she murmured, progressing with the wash in the same haphazard way as if she were cutting the grass in the back garden. Her late husband had pulled her up on her erratic mowing often enough. Yes, his life had been very ordered. But he had never been able to make her conform to his ways. Half the thrill of her single extra-marital adventure had derived from her wilful transgression against his pedantry. But the other half, she reminded herself, eyes closed and with soapy hands cupping her breasts and gently thumbing her nipples to erection, that was pure delectation, not to be eclipsed, as she thought at the time.

That was before she met Rudolf. The longstanding affair with him started a couple of years after Erika had been widowed. All the same, she thought, he would not have been to late husband Herbert's liking. "A silver-tongued smoothie, and a marriage wrecker," he would have summed Rudolf up, had he ever met him.

Erika sighed: 'marriage wrecker' held unpleasant connotations for herself. Her affair with Rudolf had turned out to be the last straw as far as Rudolf's wife was concerned and led to separation and eventually to the break-up of their marriage.

Anyway, it was not something she wanted to dwell on right now, and she pushed thoughts of part-responsibility quickly out of her mind.

Letting her fingers slide over the silky white skin of hips and belly, Erika day-dreamed of Rudolf's sensual touch. It would not be long now. In about an hour he would step over the threshold and back into her life. "See you tomorrow at eight," his note had said.

The fact that he had thrown her over when Anni came on the scene had hurt her feelings and also knocked her pride. But she had made light of it. Well, she mocked, it wasn't as if Rudolf was her one and only love. Was he now? Nevertheless, he had treated her badly and she had the right to feel angry.

So when, a couple of days ago, he appeared on her doorstep, brazenly intending to refresh their relationship after Anni's escape to the West, Erika had been stunned. When he invited her out for dinner as if everything was normal between them and they were still lovers she just about managed to snort, "You've got a nerve!" before slamming the front door shut right in his face.

He called on her again the next evening but she did not answer the door. She had stood behind it, silently fuming. Assuming she could hear him he had begged to be let in, saying, "Give me a minute and at least listen to what I have to say. Please, for old time's sake."

Later, after he had gone away her fury had softened. No way had she forgiven him. Oh, no! But she could not deny that a relationship with Rudolf had its compensations. Life without him, she granted, had been rather drab. When he turns up again, as he had said he would – in the note he left behind – she was going to let him into the house, tell him in no uncertain terms what she thought of his behaviour, and only after a decent interval would she be persuaded to succumb to his charm. As far as her emotions were concerned, she would keep them well under control. She would play it cool. She was confident that she could pull it off. Why shouldn't she make the best of the situation and enjoy herself? Life was for living, and once she got old and wrinkly she would have saucy memories to lighten her days. In any case, should she waver at any time and let her feelings gain the upper hand, all she needed to do was to remind herself of Anni. It would surely bring her down to earth.

While Erika lay awake for hours she pondered the whys and wherefores of Rudolf coming back to her. She did not doubt that that was what he wanted to do. He would not take the trouble merely to explain himself. No, not Rudolf.

She eventually came to the conclusion that he had seen sense.

Taking up with Anni must have been some sort of aberration on Rudolf's part.

It had probably something to do with vanity. After all what did he have in common with a girl half his age? What would they have talked about?

Now she, Erika, and Rudolf had plenty to say to each other. And the physical side of their relationship could not have been better. She had nothing to fear in that respect. No, nothing at all.

But at the thought of Rudolf and Anni in bed together, as they undoubtedly had been, a jaundiced expression ran momentarily over Erika's face, as if she had bitten into a green lemon. But she did not allow jealousy to take hold. Instead, a smile of victory formed on her lips as she reminded herself that that girl had chosen to leave. Things could not have been perfect in *that* department.

As Erika daintily stepped onto the bathmat she saw herself reflected in the full-length mirror. Prancing about on pedicured feet and looking at her tight stomach and full bosom, she judged that Rudolf was sure to compliment her on her appearance, as well as be bound to notice the expensive scent of lavender on her skin.

Only last night Frau B had visited to deliver Erika's latest order consisting of lavender soap and eyeshadow. "I've not been home yet, I'm coming straight from the station to you," Frau B said, as she clomped in soil-encrusted rubber boots into the living room of Erika's little cottage, "I've not even taken the time to have a cup of coffee."

"Right," said Erika, "I'll put the kettle on. Could do with a cuppa myself, only just arrived home from work. But where are the western goodies I ordered?"

Frau B did not answer. Instead she first unbuttoned and then slipped out of her worn rabbit pelt coat, before lifting her skirt and pulling it up to her chin. From a strong leather belt, fixed over the waistline of her slip, hung several strong canvas bags. With her right hand Frau B got hold of one of the two front ones and, teasingly, pulled it to and fro like a pendulum. Then, having unclipped it from the belt, she raised the heavy-seeming receptacle into the air as if it were the trophy of a decapitated head. "They're in here," she said proudly. "The police never even checked me at the border." She smiled regally, and allowing her eyelids to flutter for a few seconds, she continued, "Well, I put on my mental retard act." For demonstration, Frau B let her jaw drop, managing to set the open mouth sideways with lolling tongue drooling saliva. The utterance she produced was unfathomable.

Anyway, Erika had burst out laughing – with Frau B joining in, once she had massaged her jaw back into position.

The manner in which Frau B made a living was a well-kept secret. Two or three times a month she visited her daughter in East Berlin, avowedly to help with the children. While there, she would slip across to the West, exchange East Mark for the Western currency, at the rate of five to one, and make the purchases on behalf of her clients, buying quality goods unavailable back home.

Her coup de grace had been the cross-border transportation of a pair of skies in the middle of summer. Once in the West she had retrieved them from the luggage rack – where they had lain unclaimed by all the passengers when a border guard asked whose they were – and packed and posted them on to a friend's son in Heidelberg. She liked talking about this knockout accomplishment, and each time she did so, her cheeks would glow and her voice become breathless. The secret of her success apparently was that she, the rotund middle-aged woman, who habitually transformed herself into a feeble-minded half-wit, did not, in the eyes of the guardians of the GDR, pose a security threat.

At a quarter to eight Erika was ready for Rudolf. Carefully dressed, her face made up, she paced through the rooms of her cottage, fluffing up a cushion here, moving a chair there and re-arranging the coffee cups on the living room couch table. With ten minutes to go she positioned herself at the window of her unlit bedroom from where she could overlook his approach.

It was not the first time she had spied on him in this way; his stance and manner of walk had told her much about his state of mind and so given her advance intelligence. Towards the end of their relationship she had come to be disconcerted by his slow, hesitant steps. In the early days it seemed that he could not get to her place fast enough, and on his arrival they had not wasted time on polite how-do you-dos but torn off their clothes en route to the bedroom.

Looking out into the cold late November night, the street was devoid of vehicles. The only person she could see out there was stumbling along towards her. Surely a drunk, she thought. Who else would push as unconcernedly right through the large pothole opposite her house? She noted the oily, rainbow-coloured water ripple in the moonlight once he had crossed the jagged hollow.

It occurred to her that there was something familiar about the man as he stopped to pull out a bottle from the deep pocket of his coat. Facing her cottage, he raised the bottle as if in a greeting before setting it to his lips. It was then that she remembered having given Herbert's coat to that needy man when he came to her door about a week ago.

Erika watched the vagrant until he disappeared from her field of vision. There was still no sign of Rudolf though. Was he playing hard to get? Don't worry, she told herself, he'll be here.

Had it not been for his wife's frozen shoulder, she would probably never have met Rudolf. In her capacity as a hospital physiotherapist, Erika accepted the odd private assignment – one of which had been the treatment of Frau Darrenbach's said frozen shoulder.

Erika had been on her second visit to Frau Darrenbach when, according to Rudolf, on his arrival home one evening, he had heard strange noises, a sort of grunting, which had drawn him to investigate.

Upon entering the marital bedroom, he had found his partly clothed wife lying prone on the bed and bent over her was a second female in a white coat, engaged in vigorous massaging. Surprised by the spectacle, he had stopped dead in his tracks. The unknown woman's shapely legs, clad in black, seamed stockings, came into glorious view each time she bent low whence her coat rose up to thigh level. He eventually – to the consternation of both women – had given his presence away when he could not stop a sneeze.

Because he very much liked what he had ogled at, he suggested, at the end of the therapy session, to accompany Erika on her way home in the dark as she lived at the edge of the town.

However, since she had arrived in her second-hand Trabant, she refused his offer.

Aware of his attraction for her and her own interest in him, Erika made sure not to be mobile the next time she visited her lady patient.

Rudolf, for his part, staged one of his rare stay-at-home evenings when Erika next called. Pretending to suffer from a headache and needing fresh air, he again offered Erika his company.

After much coaxing from both Darrenbachs, she accepted.

Having made a speedy, miraculous recovery, he invited her for a drink on the way to her cottage.

Suffice it to say, before his wife's treatment was completed, Rudolf and Erika were lovers.

To allay Erika's scruples concerning Rudolf's unfaithfulness he assured her that she, Erika, was not taking anything from his wife since their relationship was entirely platonic. Besides, they had both agreed to an open marriage, he said.

To her cost, Erika was to learn otherwise.

Some time after Frau Darrenbach's completed treatment, the latter sought Erika out in the hospital, confronted her in one of the corridors and slapped her face.

"You know," said Rudolf's wife after the attack, while looking almost pityingly at Erika, "he'll throw you over just like that," and she clicked finger and thumb. "Wait and see how you'll feel then." Probing Erika's face, Frau Darrenbach remarked, "You're my age. All it takes is a younger floozie, eh?" The triumph in Frau Darrenbach's voice served to remind Erika that she too was the wrong side of forty.

※

The instant Erika's mantle clock in the living room began to strike eight times, she saw Rudolf walking towards her cottage, as he had promised in yesterday's note. He walked without haste, but purposefully. After avoiding the puddle near her front door he stopped momentarily, straightened his tie and drew a comb through his long dark hair. In the light of her porch she saw that his lips were moving as if he were rehearsing a prepared speech.

Feeling pleased, she went to the front door and waited. When the bell rang, she first counted to twenty before opening it.

"Shut the door behind you and come to the living room," she said, smiling sweetly. She was wearing the black cocktail dress he favoured, black stockings and stiletto-heeled shoes. Walking in front of him, she wiggled her voluptuous bottom, which she knew he had always found seductive.

"Sit yourself down," she said, pointing to a group of easy chairs. "Coffee's made." She disappeared into the kitchen and on her return she poured the steaming liquid.

She lowered herself into the chair opposite his and fixed her blue eyes on him, but she did not speak. Surely, it was his turn first. But instead of apologising profusely, he sipped from his cup.

His nonchalance threw her somewhat. Had he not been rehearsing a prepared speech only minutes before? Furthermore, there was no sign that he had brought her one of his 'little presents'. In the past, after a tiff, he would smooth the waves and present her with one more silver charm for her bracelet. Also, he knew how much she liked flowers!

As the seconds ticked away in silence, the sweet smile left her face; and to cover her disappointment it now took on a haughty expression. She looked at him combatively. But too preoccupied with her own feelings, she did not notice the hardening of his features in response.

"You know," he said – having taken in and objecting to what he took to be her arrogant demeanour – and came straight to the point, "when I made the excuses that I was too busy to see you, I was courting Anni."

Erika flinched.

Realising that he had been too abrupt, he tried to make amends. "I should have told you, instead of blaming it all on the clocks. I'm sorry you had to hear about it from others."

Erika's feelings were in turmoil. You're not sorry, she thought. The only person you are sorry for is you. Why have you come here? I didn't think it was to hurt me. She frowned but kept herself in check.

"We'd been together for a long time," he continued, "and you deserved better. But to be fair to myself," he smiled as he touched his chest, "when I was ready to tell you about it, you refused to listen. Remember?"

"So, you thought to keep me in reserve," Erika said coolly – icy might be a more apt description.

"Well," Rudolf started, "I didn't know if Anni—"

"Never mind all that now," Erika interrupted him.

Fuck your Anni, she thought and felt a red-hot prickling sensation rise up. If you know what is good for you, you don't mention that name again! But, in a last ditch heroic effort at reconciliation, she took a deep breath.

She leaned back in her chair. She crossed her legs, showing an ample length of thigh. She even managed a smile again.

Satisfied that she could still entice Rudolf – the twinkle of old showed in his eyes – she felt a surge of power. She fancied that this very moment he was thinking of the fun-times he had been missing. She also knew how much he'd enjoyed her gossip and taking the mickey out of the townsfolk. He'd told her often enough.

Seeing his features soften and his body relax, she gave in to the temptation of paying him back, just a little, for his betrayal. "What did you expect from that slip of a girl?" she mocked. "The whole thing was just a laugh for her. How could you be so stupid?"

He did not answer, and exhilarated by her aggression and, what she took to be his admission of guilt, she did not notice the twitching of his mouth, a sure sign of his mounting anger.

Having assumed the moral high ground she was enjoying herself. Sitting up and pushing her chest out, and with head and nose held high, she continued to mock, "That girl was bound to dump you." Her blue eyes glistened and she seemed to smell a scent of conquest in the air. "She—"

"Shut up!" red-faced, Rudolf interrupted her before she could go on. "You don't know *anything*, so don't jump to conclusions."

Erika's temper got the better of her and she shouted back, "I would've thought you'd be glad to be shot of her. Why come to me if you're not?"

But even as she was hollering at Rudolf, she thought it was all going wrong. If only she could have pushed the image of younger Anni out of her mind!

Anyway, after Erika's torrents of language, Rudolf lost control. He jumped to his feet, and in the heat of the moment, he roared, "I'm through with you! I don't have to listen to you slagging off Anni."

As Rudolf stormed out of the room, one of Erika's shoes thudded into the doorframe behind him. "Fuck you too," she sneered.

❦

Erika just stood there, looking at the doorframe, and the shoe, and back, again and again. She felt utterly deflated.

It dawned on her that she had not been honest with herself. Her motive for giving Rudolf a second chance had been more serious than the professed quest for enjoyment and fun. If that had been all she wanted, she would not smart the way she now did. What was more, fury towards Rudolf and self-deception, the remedies she had used to get over her first rejection, were no longer any good to her.

She could see that the decision to play it cool had been a sham, while in her heart she had harboured hopes for a lasting relationship, marriage even, with Rudolf, now that he was free.

As she continued staring at the doorframe and her shoe, the truth sank in: any hopes for permanency with Rudolf were now dead. There was no going back.

To add insult to injury, she kept reliving the horrid spectacle that had just been played out. Eventually, she forced herself to turn around and move away.

Seeing herself in the hall mirror, she impulsively clawed at her expensive black dress. She laughed hysterically as she pulled it over her head, hearing the seam at the back rip. "Okay!" she shouted, and tore the dress from top to bottom. "Let me do it properly." She knew she would never again wear it. In disgust she threw the mutilated dress to the floor and stamped on it.

Erika was still agitated as she got out a pair of scissors

from her needlework basket and started to cut the silk tie she had bought for Rudolf into tiny shreds.

For a fleeting moment a – for her – monstrous thought flashed through her mind: she could tell on Rudolf. It would only take a word into Stasi-ears and her revenge would be complete. She knew where Rudolf kept his Western magazines and newspapers. He had even got hold of fashion magazines for her.

No! Erika shuddered at having considered the idea. She was not going to sink so low as to become a fucking informer! Besides, it would entangle Frau B. True, newspapers of any kind were the one thing Frau B did not deal in. "Black market trading is one thing," she had told Erika, "but no way am I going to get involved with politics." But once *they* searched Rudolf's flat, questions about his silk shirts with the Western labels would be asked. The Stasi would have a field day going through his belongings. They would find out about his supplier. Imagining Frau B being pulled in for questioning made Erika feel quite ill. Acting the fool here in her Aschersleben hometown would not work for Frau B, especially since she had been a schoolteacher for many years.

For the next hour or so, Erika kept pacing through her cottage. Noticing that she was shivering in her underwear, she wrapped herself in a woollen dressing gown. She poured herself a glass of schnapps before fetching the bottle of Russian Sekt from the cooler. Having managed to open the bottle, with some difficulty, she gulped two glasses of the sparkling stuff straight down. The rest of the bottle she drank more leisurely, every so often raising her glass and saying 'cheers' to an imaginary Frau Darrenbach. How right she had been!

# *Willi*

## *Ulterior Motives*

Waking up after last night's reunion with Rudolf, Willi felt terrible. His head was pounding and he felt nauseous. Right there and then he vowed never again to get as 'sloshed' as he had got last night in that godforsaken pub. Rubbing his eyes and groaning, he rolled over onto his right side.

The little clock on his coffee table showed twenty minutes past ten. But that was nothing to worry about, it being Sunday morning.

Very slowly, Willy pushed his legs sideways. Once they were overhanging the edge of the living-room sofa, he propped himself up on his elbow into a semi-sitting position. Letting gravity work for him, his feet touched the floor and his upper half yanked fully upright.

He remained perched on the side of the sofa, wishing that the pulsating in his temples would stop. It didn't. No matter how much pressure he applied.

Careful not to make any sudden move, he looked around. Why wasn't he in his bed? How did he get to lie on the sofa, still dressed...? Willi had no clue. Even worse, he couldn't remember getting home.

"Shit, shit, shit," he said, first in a whisper, then louder. Shifting his weight, he groaned once more.

He had met Rudolf shortly after eight in that out-of-the way pub. What was it called again? Well, what does it matter? Anyway, he had written the name down somewhere.

It hadn't been his choice, he would have preferred a place with a bit more go in the centre of East Berlin.

Allowing plenty of time to find the obscure Gasthaus, Willi had got there forty minutes early. He was keen to meet Rudolf and didn't mind waiting. What he wanted to avoid was being late and missing Rudolf.

When Willi's former colleague had written and proposed the meeting, Willi had agreed straightaway. That was despite the fact that Rudolf had distanced himself for at least a year before he left Berlin to live in the provinces.

The truth was that Willi greatly admired Rudolf and was only too ready to make allowances: maybe it hadn't been an excuse and Rudolf really didn't have the time to socialise with him?

Anyway, apart from being flattered by Rudolf's newly ignited interest, Willi was intrigued. How could he be 'of help'? – that was one of the phrases Rudolf had used in his letter.

If it were the case that Rudolf was planning to come back to the capital city, Willi would gladly put in a good word, now that he had some influence. What was the point of holding power if it couldn't be used to benefit an old chum? And, just maybe, in the process he would learn to emulate Rudolf's easy-going manner and charm.

Joining the SED – the GDR's ruling party – had certainly given Willi a leg up on the job ladder. No longer was he a nobody in the office. It was he who gave the orders now. Hence Rudolf would not have any problems in getting his old position back. He, Willi, would make sure of it. And if Rudolf were to listen and take an example…well, the sky would be the limit…

The thought of belonging to the inner circle of Rudolf's friends again and to live the excitement of the old days had filled Willi with joy. So, as he waited in the pub for his former colleague to arrive he had started to toast the good things to come. Only, in anticipation, he had rather overdone the celebratory drinks.

When Rudolf finally arrived, half an hour late, Willi, his flushed face beaming, greeted his former colleague and steered him to the table he had been sitting at, meting out some hearty backslaps in the process.

And it has to be said, by this time, Willi had convinced himself that Rudolf really was planning to come back to East Berlin. Willi could see it all, just as in the past, Rudolf's success with the ladies would rub off… . With Rudolf around, he, Willi, would once more meet the kind of women he desired but never managed to get close to under his own steam.

Levering himself up, Willi rose from the unfamiliar sleeping quarter and made his way on stockinged feet to the bathroom. A look into the mirror made him gasp at his reflection. Christ, didn't he look like white beer and spit!

Splashing cold water on his face made him feel a little better.

Later, having tidied himself up and after swallowing two

aspirins, he sat in his kitchen, sipping strong black coffee. Snippets of last night's conversation surfaced from the blur of his memories.

"Why move to the provinces?" Willi heard himself ask. And had he not suggested to Rudolf that it must have been because of woman trouble?

But ignoring Willi's intimation, Rudolf had insisted that he had only moved to the small town of Aschersleben, situated at the foot of the Harz Mountains, for the business premises.

As if! Willi had thought, unconvinced.

Willi drunk some more coffee and lit a cigarette. In his mind's eye he saw Rudolf's exquisite face. No wonder women fell under his spell. He dazzled them with his bright grey eyes, the longish, very dark hair, and the skin of Mediterranean appearance. In addition, he was tall and slim, always well dressed and carefully groomed.

For a moment, Willi pushed his chin out. *I'm as tall*, he thought, and defiantly he straightened up on his stool. *I've got a good head of hair. I'm even a little younger, only forty-two. Okay, maybe not as slim. Why can't I pull the birds?*

Rudolf had once told him that the secret was not to be tentative, "Go in with all guns blazing," he had said. "And don't be accommodating. Know what you want and take it."

At the time, Willi thought that he had detected a glint of ice in Rudolf's eyes as he dished out his advice. But seeing the charming smile that followed it had made Willi doubt himself. No, he must have misunderstood…cruelty wasn't Rudolf's thing, was it?

Relaxing his chin again and taking up his usual slouched manner of sitting on the kitchen stool, it crossed Willi's mind that there had been other occasions when Rudolf's words and the facial expressions that went with them had been at variance.

*I don't actually know what makes Rudolf tick,* Willi thought. *A bit of an enigma, this guy…*

Last night for example, before he got pissed out of his mind, Willi had noticed derision in Rudolf's eyes. Yet, had Rudolf not nodded agreement as he, Willi, extolled the virtue of joining the *Party*? "It was the best thing I ever did," he remembered saying. "Go on, give it a go." And he had added that not being bothered about politics need not be an obstacle, confiding that he wasn't interested in dogma either.

"Bloody drink," Willi swore. It had turned the rest of the evening into a nebulous mist. One thing though still stood out. Rudolf had referred to 'turning over a new leaf'. What had he meant? Well, it must have been to do with returning to the capital. What else?

The bell shrilled and cut off any further speculating.

※

"Who the hell's that?" Willi grumbled. "On a Sunday." But he stuck his feet into leather slippers and headed to the door. "I'm coming," he shouted, as the bell rang out again, and while he buttoned up his shirt. Maybe it was Rudolf? Mollified by the possibility, he started whistling.

"Who are you?" Willi asked, once he had pulled the door to his flat open.

"You won't remember me," a youngish man in shorts and matching top said. "I'm the taxi driver from last night. Fritz Koch is my name." Seeing Willi's uncomprehending face, he gave a little smile. "Just as I thought, you don't remember me."

"Taxi driver?" Willi repeated; he was none the wiser.

"God, you were tight, of that I can assure you. We had to carry you. Absolutely legless you were."

The man smiled more broadly. "You were snoring all the way. Like a pig, if you'll excuse my French." He fumbled in the pocket of his top and pulled something small out. "Your address book," he said, offering it. "I found it on the back seat."

"Oh," said Willi. "Thank you. I'm very obliged. Haven't started missing the thing. Only just got up."

"Well, I'll be off then. Tschüs."

"No, wait," said Willi. "Please come in for a minute. Where are my manners?" *If I don't sit down, I'll fall down,* he thought and led the way to his living room. The address book was essential to him. Apart from the contact details of family and friends, it held those of his co-committee members and Party comrades. Then there were important birthday dates he had noted down.

*I wonder,* Willi thought, *is this Fritz Koch aware of who I am? If he's gone through the booklet he must know. But he behaves quite normal, no deference, no hostility…*

"How did you sleep?" the man asked, pointing to the sofa.

"Ach, the less said, the better." Willi sighed. "But tell me, you said 'we', I mean who else apart from you carried me in here?"

"He said his name was Rudolf. Mean anything to you?"

Willi nodded, looking puzzled.

"Dear oh dear," said last night's driver, "you really don't remember anything! You kept fumbling about for your door keys, he took them from you. I helped him get you up the stairs. You grunted as we laid you down, and you started that awful snoring again."

"Can I offer you anything?' Willi pulled off a half-smile. "I have fruit juice, you know."

The man declined.

After confirming that Willi did not owe money for the fare, Willi nevertheless went to fetch his wallet from his jacket. It still was where Fritz Koch had flung it the night before, over the back of a chair.

On Willi's insistence, the man accepted fifty marks in recompense for his time and trouble. On parting, at the door, Willi casually observed, "I trust you and Rudolf had an uneventful trip to his hotel."

Fritz Koch stopped in his tracks. "What hotel?" He turned to Willi, "Rudolf stayed behind here, with you." Shaking his head, Fritz Koch departed.

❦

Willi went back to the kitchen and put the kettle on.

Over a fresh cup of coffee, he tried to make sense of Rudolf having apparently stayed behind. Why would he have done such a thing? For how long was he here? There was nothing objectionable about him staying on. After all, he had an open invitation for bed and breakfast. But why disappear before morning and without any explanation?

With the taxi gone, Rudolf would have had to ring for another one – from here it was a hell of a walk to *Der Grüne Baum*, the hotel Rudolf had said he was staying at.

Well, it was all very odd, Willi decided. Then, chuckling to himself, he wondered: what if Rudolf had needed a shit? But Willi immediately disregarded that idea. Surely, Rudolf would have asked the driver to wait.

"Curious and curiouser," Willi mused after his telephone call to *Der Grüne Baum*. The receptionist had no knowledge of Herr Rudolf Darrenbach staying at the hotel. "No, sorry," she said, "he's not booked in with us."

Willi then rang Rudolf's Aschersleben number. But he got no reply.

Willi resolved he would try again later – to allow more time for Rudolf to have returned home prematurely from his Berlin trip.

For some reason, Rudolf's whereabouts had become something of an obsession to Willi, even though he asked himself: *what is it to me? After eighteen months of being ignored, I'm behaving like a mother hen. More likely than not, Rudolf made another conquest and is at this moment being spoiled with home cooking.*

At the thought of a roast with all the trimmings, Willi shook himself. Dry toast would do him for his meal.

Around five, when Willi telephoned Rudolf again, there was still no answer. On the off chance, he tried the workshop number.

A woman's voice answered. "Rudolf, where are you?" she said, before Willi could open his mouth. "I've been trying you everywhere."

Disconcerted, Willi asked to speak to his former colleague.

There was a long pause before the voice informed him that Rudolf was not 'available'.

What did that mean? Anyway, Willi wasn't going to give up easily. He explained who he was and said that he had met Rudolf the night before. At the mention of Rudolf in Berlin, the woman started sobbing.

It later transpired that Willi had got through to Doris who urgently needed to speak to Rudolf as the next day the two of them were going on their planned holiday to the Baltic coast. Only Rudolf was nowhere to be found. He had even changed all the locks, and she had climbed through a back window to get into the workshop. She kept saying, "Why? What is happening? I can't understand any of it."

After putting the receiver down, the only thing Willi could think of doing was to invite himself round to Astrid for the evening.

She lived within twenty minutes walk of him. She was a good friend and a colleague. She also knew Rudolf, though not in the biblical sense, as she had jokingly said.

If anybody could make sense of the goings-on, it was she. Amongst the office staff she had the reputation of being an agony aunt. Not that I have a personal problem, Willi said to himself, but he felt a yearning to be near her.

Willi remembered her flat from before. It was about a year ago that he had last visited it. The living-room furniture was the same. The genuine but worn Afghan carpet was still in place, as were the velvet curtains.

How lovely and cosy it is here, Willi thought, as he sat down on one end of the settee.

By the time Astrid brought in a tray with lemon tea and black bread sandwiches, Willi felt relaxed enough to have shut his eyes for a few minutes.

"Sorry," he apologised, "it's been a bit busy."

Astrid didn't say anything but gave him a warm smile. "I'll be mother," she said and started pouring the tea.

As Willi looked on, he saw her in a new light. Why hadn't he noticed her attractive looks before? 'Homely' was what Rudolf had called her. How off the mark that was! For the first time, Willi wondered whether Rudolf's belittlement had been enough to make him discount her as a possible conquest.

"You'd better tell me what's troubling you," Astrid said, encouraging him with another warm smile. "You didn't let on earlier…"

As she bent forward to pass him one of the steaming cups, he breathed in a whiff of the Nivea soap she obviously still favoured. He remembered that he had always found the scent pleasant, not at all 'primitive' as Rudolf claimed.

"Last night Rudolf and I celebrated," Willi started. And he went on to recount all he remembered about their pub reunion. He talked about the visit of Fritz Koch this morning and related what Doris had said on the telephone.

Afterwards, Astrid sat for a long time in silence, seemingly deep in thought. Every so often she was biting her bottom lip.

"You know..." she eventually said. "I've got an idea..." Combing her fingers through her short dark hair, she looked Willi straight in the eyes. "I apologise if I'm doing Rudolf an injustice, but..." She hesitated again, then asked, "Have you noticed anything missing at home?"

"How do you mean?" he uttered, perplexed.

"Well..." Astrid blushed. "I'm sorry to say I don't trust Rudolf. I have my reasons...but I won't go into that now. I suspect he had an ulterior motive."

Willi looked as perplexed as before. "I don't understand..."

"Think about it," she said: "Rudolf suddenly turns up, doesn't give a solid reason... . Well, not a good enough one, after he'd dropped you."

Realising that Willi's raised arm meant that he was about to jump to Rudolf's defence, she just said, "Let's call a spade a spade. Okay?"

Willi looked away.

"He knows," she continued, "in spite of the way he treated you, you're still in awe of him and you're bound to agree to a meeting. So, what does he do? He makes the arrangements and gets you drunk. Listen," Astrid said, drawing Willi's gaze, "I think he planned it all carefully. He takes you home, stays behind in your flat. Why?"

Giving Willi a knowing smile, she quipped, "He didn't do your washing-up, or your carpet cleaning, did he now?"

A glint of hostility came into her eyes: "He had an ulterior motive all right. I'm sure of it. Rudolf looks after number one."

Turning her face away from Willi, she whispered, "I'm glad I didn't give in to him. It would have been on his terms… . This Doris must be heartbroken…"

It dawned on Willi. "Rudolf," he started, "well, he made me think he didn't fancy you, not in that way. He…"

"Is that what he said?" But brushing away any answer Willi might give, Astrid suggested that he check his flat for anything missing. "And I don't mean money," she said.

"But I haven't got anything Rudolf would want."

"I'd say you have," Astrid told Willi. "Check your desk, or wherever you keep your papers. I suspect he's done a runner to the West. I should imagine it would be easy carrying your documents."

She came over to sit next to Willi on the settee. "You don't know how refreshing it is to be with you," she said and took his hand into hers. "At heart you're an innocent."

Ten days later Willi received a small package from West Berlin. It contained his tampered-with Identity Pass, – the photograph in it was that of Rudolf – Party membership documents as well as official letters from various committees.

In the accompanying note, Rudolf thanked Willi for the loan of the documents, mentioning how invaluable they had been in enabling him to 'turn over a new leaf'.

Willi was horrified. How could Rudolf have done such

a thing? He must have known – or should have known – what the consequences for Willi might be. After all, the chances were high that the package would be intercepted. Could Rudolf hate him that much? No, surely not.

Rocking forward and backward in his leather captain's chair, Willi eventually decided that sending the documents back just had to have been an ill-judged practical joke on Rudolf's part. Nobody would do such a thing except to the worst enemy!

In his quandary, Willi kept picking up the wretched note from his desk. Holding it with sweaty hands, he repeatedly asked himself: *what the heck am I going to do?*

Wait and see was one option. Maybe his luck was in and the delivery had gone unnoticed? After a few weeks without being pulled in for questioning he could pretend that he had lost his pass, report it to the police and be issued with a replacement.

Being in the pickle he was, Willi forgot about time and place. He should have left for the office ten minutes ago.

This morning he would be late. But that is the least of my worries, he thought. None of his colleagues would reprimand him, the manager.

Holding his head in his hands, Willi groaned. If only he could turn the clock back. Why didn't he report the loss of his documents days ago after he first noticed that they were missing? Why didn't he listen to Astrid and voice his – at any rate her – suspicions about Rudolf? If he had, he would be in the clear now.

Then he had an idea. Why not make capital out of the returned items? Providing nothing untoward was to happen, he could do a bit of DIY to replace Rudolf's photograph in the identity pass. He, Willi, had nimble fingers, didn't he? As an additional bonus, doing the repair work would keep rebuke from Astrid at bay. For, on that Sunday evening, he had reluctantly agreed with her on the course of action to take, should he, on his return home, find his papers missing. "I'll definitely report the theft to the police," he had vouched, all the while thinking that Astrid's suspicion of Rudolf was bound to be unfounded.

But when she had been proved right, he had not kept his promise. Scruples, indecision, even laziness had prevented him from acting on it. So he had put it off from one day to the next.

He knew that Astrid would be furious to learn of his omission. But if he fixed the problem of his missing photograph she need never find out.

Envisaging a possible solution to his problem, he was beginning to feel more optimistic and he recalled last night's outing with Astrid. After his invitation to a performance of the *Swan Lake* ballet, he had taken her to dinner. A very agreeable date it had turned out to be. A glow came to his face, and he even managed to gloss over the embarrassing fact that he had told a blatant lie. "Oh yes," he had answered her, "the matter of those documents, no need to worry…" His words had been accompanied by sweeping gestures of his arms – of a type, he fancied, a man of the world would deliver. It was copied from Rudolf.

The next morning, as Willi stepped out of the building, he was led, politely, to a waiting limousine. "You are required at headquarters," said one of the two smartly dressed men, and took him by the arm.

Willi's built-up hopes collapsed. All he could think of was Rudolf's damned package. It seemed Rudolf had dropped him in it. It could be nothing else, could it?

"Good morning, Karl," Willi said, deliberately cheerful, as he walked jauntily into the room of the Party Secretary. The two men were on first-name terms and regularly met for a pint in the nearby *Das Weisse Ross*.

When Karl ignored Willi's outstretched hand, Willi knew he was in serious trouble.

"Sit down, Herr Schell," Karl said. And as if not to leave Willi in any doubt at all, he added, "I am Herr Stiefel."

At that, Willi could not stifle a somewhat hysterical giggle. Karl pretended not to hear and busied himself with a bulky file.

As he turned the pages, he occasionally peered over the top of his glasses at Willi, shaking his head as he did so.

"So, you abetted Rudolf Darrenbach by letting him use your papers…to enable him to…" Karl slapped the file down on the desk. "A clear-cut case of accessory to commit the crime of *Republikflucht*. Whatever were you thinking of! I'm very much afraid Rudolf's gratitude will cost you dearly." Karl smirked. "Who needs enemies with friends like that?" he asked sweetly.

"You've got it all wrong," Willi said. "My friend, Astrid, from the office – you know her – she will tell you what happened."

"I see, another friend." This time it was Karl who giggled.

Willi ignored the wisecrack. "Rudolf stole my papers. I didn't give them to him. I was out for the count. The taxi driver will confirm that. He and Rudolf bundled me indoors, and Rudolf stayed behind. That's when he fixed himself up with my pass. His photo was still in it when he sent it back."

In his agitation, Willi had got to his feet. He was pacing the room, then abruptly stopped. "Karl," he said, slumping back into his chair, "I'm telling you the truth. You know me, I wouldn't help anyone to escape, being a loyal Party member. You must know that."

"I don't know any such thing, Herr Schell," said Karl.

"Please," Willi begged, "believe me. When I told Astrid about the reunion with Rudolf and how pissed I got and how I was taken home and that Rudolf stayed behind in my flat, she right away smelled a rat. Told me to check if anything was missing…" Willy paused to draw breath.

"And did you… check I mean?" Karl sounded amused.

"That's when I noticed the documents missing. Astrid had been right all along."

Karl picked up the file again, leafed through it. "Nothing here about a theft."

For a moment Willi's face crumpled, suggestive of a cartoon character. "I was going to report it. I told Astrid that I would… . But you know how it is…" He lifted his arms up, before letting them sink into his lap.

Willi knew it looked bad for him. He was desperately trying to think of an explanation for his stupidity. For that was what it amounted to. He could see it now. If only…

Someone in uniform had entered the room and approached Karl's chair. The police officer proceeded to crouch on his haunches, before whispering something into Karl's ear.

"Aha!" Karl hissed triumphantly in response. "We've got him now." With the policeman in tow, he hurried to the door. But about halfway, he turned back and picked up the file from his desk.

Presently Willi found himself locked in. Gloom enveloped him. What was the significance of the interrupted interview? What had Karl meant? Had they searched his flat and found other evidence against him, Willi? The unanswered questions weighted him down.

About an hour later, the policeman returned without Karl. He handcuffed Willi, before delivering him to, what Willi later learned was, a prison for suspects awaiting trial. He had been blindfolded, so he could not see where he was being taken.

He was placed into a cell two metres by three. Very high up was a tiny window of dull frosted glass. A bench with a mattress, a bucket and a sink completed the inventory. Through the spy-hole in the thick door, a guard watched.

For the next two weeks he was kept in solitary confinement. There were no telephone calls, no lawyer, no contact with the outside world. Sleep deprivation was the method used to make him talk. Every night he was interrogated for six hours. During the day he was not permitted to sleep. A guard watched through the peephole and made sure he didn't sleep.

Willi lost all sense of time, he became disorientated. All he wanted to do was sleep, sleep.

In the end, Willi gave his interrogator – sometimes there were two of them – what he wanted to hear. Yes, he had helped Rudolf. And yes, he was preparing for his own escape.

From the way the questioning was going, Willi had gathered that his flat had been searched. His Identity Pass minus Rudolf's photograph had been found in his desk, together with a photo of himself, which he had already clipped onto the space where his picture had been in the first place.

After his admission, Willi was allowed to sleep for three whole days and nights.

The judge sentenced him to twenty-four months imprisonment, and by the time Willi was released, the Berlin

Wall was an established reality – Walter Ulbricht called it an 'anti-fascist protective measure': Easterners had to be kept safe from criminals.

Willi's dispiriting prison days – they started at 4.30 and he was made to work in a sweatshop gluing envelopes – were made bearable by Astrid's sporadic visits. Sporadic, because her applications to visit were frequently refused.

"You know of course that you turn yourself into a leper by coming here?" Willi had reminded her when she first came to see him.

"I know the truth," she said, "that's what matters."

Tonight, six months after his discharge from prison, Willi was once again relaxing in Astrid's cosy flat, sipping lemon tea from the cup she had handed him.

Being enveloped in her warm gaze, he was more convinced than ever that he had maintained his sanity only because of her steadfast support. She had made it possible for him to dream...

That dream was about to come true. Tomorrow they were going to be married.

*Bloc II*

# Fräulein Vogel

## Weathering the Storm

Carmen Vogel and the rest of the tenants had come together to see the Russians move into town. Watching from a first-floor window of their Wallenstein Street building, they witnessed the latest wave of troops taking possession of Aschersleben.

The townsfolk had been much relieved when at the end of the war, back in April, the Americans had occupied them. Then, for four weeks, the British had taken over. But now, as Carmen feared, calamity was imminent.

She too had heard the dreadful stories of pillage and rape told by refugees from Silesia and East Prussia. From the Russians, so the general consensus went, no mercy could be hoped for.

Looking down into the street, Carmen saw that the common soldier looked very different from his American ally: poorly clothed, untidy and dirty. Many were pimply-faced youths. Their trucks looked uncared-for, encrusted with dirt and mud as they were. Behind the trucks came open-topped lorries, and following these were vehicles, which had dirty brown tarpaulins stretched over part of the rear. They were filled to the brim with men who were sitting on makeshift wooden benches along the sides or squatting in the middle of the floor. As they drove over the cobbled street, the soldiers were thrown about en masse – comparable, she thought, to a field of wheat tossed by a succession of sharp gusts of wind. Some of the lorries had their floors strewn with brown sacks. Straw was spilling out through the sack ends and ragged holes; some soldiers were asleep on the improvised bedding.

The Russians came in very slowly, slow enough for the horse-drawn carts to keep pace with the trucks.

Towards the end of the procession were two more vehicles with tarpaulins. They carried the wounded; some with their arms in slings, others with their heads bandaged or holding on to crutches.

Several columns of foot soldiers completed the motley band.

Compared to the dynamic way the Americans had arrived, the Russians moved in as though they were defeated troops rather than victors. There was only some heavy weaponry; most of the big stuff came in later.

With apprehension hanging in the air, Carmen and the two other women – there were also four children – said little to each other, and once the vehicles and soldiers had passed, they all went back to their own flats – Carmen's one being at the top of the building.

For the time being their new conquerors had vanished. But Carmen was under no illusion; they would be back.

Alone in her living room, she tottered aimlessly about, fidgeting with the delicate lace on her collar. She knew she ought to be doing something constructive until *they* returned. But what? Looking out of her window every few minutes certainly wasn't it…

Eventually she reminded herself that she had weathered other storms. Stay calm and carry on had been her motto when, aged twenty-five at the turn of the century, she had found herself pregnant without a husband.

It was some time since she had thought about that 'dastardly' act, for so it was seen then. Anyway, she had carried on as normal until it became difficult to hide her condition. Normal for her had been living a life of leisure at her parents' wine-growing estate.

She remembered waiting for the right time to tell her mother; until a quiet needlework evening with just the two of them together in the sitting room presented the ideal opportunity. Still, Carmen kept delaying the moment of truth. She felt as if she were perched on top of a cliff, knowing that once she took that one step over the edge, there was no going back.

In the end it was her mother who forced the issue. "Are you feeling all right, dear?" she asked. "Only you do look rather off colour lately."

"Well…yes," Carmen stammered, "but…there is something I need to tell you. I…" Having started on her confession she did not know how to continue. Under her mother's inquisitive gaze she grew beetroot-red and pale in turn.

"What is it? Come on, nobody has died."

"I might as well be dead," Carmen blurted out. "I'm pregnant!"

Her mother gave a gasp, her brows started to twitch violently. But then, to Carmen's amazement, her mother's face relaxed. "It's not all bad," she said, almost soothingly. "But I didn't think you liked Heinrich…" She hesitated as a concerned look entered her eyes, "He hasn't, or has he?"

Carmen understood. "No, of course not. It's nothing to do with *him*." There was loathing in her voice as she referred to Heinrich. Her mother ought to know better. He wouldn't even have the guts to make a pass. And surely, both her parents must have figured out that their fellow wine-grower was trying to ingratiate himself with them in the hope of winning her over.

Carmen detested the older Heinrich's silly smirk as he followed her dolefully about. There would be no problem if she carried his baby. He would marry her double quick. Certainly, her father would not object, as in time, the two estates would amalgamate…

"So, who is it if not Heinrich, hmm? There's nobody else, is there?"

But despite her mother's probing, Carmen would not divulge the name.

Called to her father's study the next day, she did not relent. His talk about her violating the family's honour and about the scandal to come did not change her mind, nor did his suggestion to meet with Heinrich and 'come to an arrangement'.

In the end, Carmen agreed to be sent to some distant relations near Stuttgart. She would stay in their village until after the birth of the baby, and then it would be placed in a nearby Catholic children's home to await adoption.

Her father soon concocted a suitable cover story for home consumption: Carmen had contracted pneumonia and recuperation in the south would become necessary. It was a convenient ploy in that the supposed poor health isolated her until her departure.

Carmen had been realistic enough to know that marriage to entertaining Marcel, a penniless seasonal estate worker from the Alsace was out of the question. She could not even claim romantic love as a mitigating circumstance for her moral lapse. It had happened in the heat of the moment during the local wine festival.

The two young people had found themselves together under the starry sky, enjoying a bottle of bubbly within the fold of a soft meadow. Marriage had been the last thing on her mind – assuming of course that Marcel was still free. And, referring to her warm-blooded nature, she had at one point during her father's inquisition, in a desperate reproach, accused him: "You shouldn't have named me 'Carmen', if you'd wanted me to be strait-laced and passionless."

When the baby was born, a beautiful boy, she named him Reinhold.

To her surprise – she had not considered herself particularly maternal – she felt unable to give him up. Her parents remonstrated with her, but without success. "You force us to disown you," they said. "The spectacle of a bastard grandchild running about the house and estate would be too much to bear."

Thinking back to her troubled days had afforded Carmen some respite from her present quandary: what was she going to do about the likely imminent return of the Russians?

Her tottering about in the living room slowed. She came altogether to a stop in front of her antique glass cabinet where, at eye level, her attention was drawn to a photo of her son as a young man – about the age Marcel had been when he had fathered Reinhold. There was a definite likeness. The same dark eyes, the same sensitive mouth. She was glad about that. So, when she picked up the silver-framed image and pressed a kiss on its mouth, it was meant for both, father and son – the memory of Marcel still held an emotional thrill, and Reinhold was, despite his advancing years, her little boy.

Until the Russians occupied the town, Carmen had been confident that she would soon be united with Reinhold – once, that is, he was released from the American POW camp he was in. Only a fortnight ago a fellow inmate had brought her news of Reinhold and told her that her son would soon be out too. But would he want to come back here, now that the situation had drastically changed?

Carmen had been ecstatic to hear that Reinhold was alive and well. He was, and always had been, her whole life. Well, except for a while when she had grown to love the likeable and liberal-minded country vet, Paul Hahn, who was willing to bring Reinhold up as his own. But it was not to be. Paul died early on in WWI, before he could take Carmen and her son away from the distant relatives near Stuttgart, where mother and son had stayed on after her refusal to give the newborn up. In return for helping in the house she was given a room, food and pocket money. Carmen was grateful. It would have been near impossible for her to support herself and the baby.

Indeed without the monthly allowance Reinhold was eventually paid by his grandparents as a goodwill gesture things would still have been dire. The money was sufficient for his needs. Carmen though was still disowned and received nothing. But, with Reinhold at boarding school, she was able to work as a live-in children's nurse. Though when her son visited her in her workplace, which was in Aschersleben, it was as her nephew. And, forever after, she and Reinhold kept up this pretence.

※

Carmen suddenly realised that she was still holding Reinhold's silver-framed photo in her hand. It was then that she sprang into action.

She could not leave the picture on view. In any forthcoming search, it would be pocketed – for the valuable frame. And what would happen to her photo album and other mementos? None of it was replaceable.

The Americans had helped themselves to pieces from the glass cabinet, but that counted little in comparison with her sentimental possessions. Where could she hide all of those?

It was dark when she carried her bag of precious things upstairs to the attic, which was used by all tenants for drying clothes and as a general storing area. Reinhold's first pair of booties fitted easily into an old shoe, which had been thrown into one corner, together with some other rubbish. The wrapped-up photos ended up under a pile of spare roof tiles, as did a miniature a passing artist had painted of Carmen when she was still a child.

Then there was her jewellery. Where was she going to hide her two diamond brooches, the pearl necklace, the rings? She thought in days to come she would need those as bargaining counters – her mother had hurriedly bundled the costly items up before Carmen was cast out. Frau Stuber, living next door, had already bartered her wedding ring in the countryside for a bag of flour with which to feed her children.

As Carmen continued searching the attic for a sanctum she remembered the loose skirting board in her bedroom. So, she took the jewellery downstairs again and prized the skirting away from the wall. Having lodged everything behind the board, she hammered the nails down.

Satisfied with her handiwork, Carmen eventually went to bed, fully clothed, That was after she had gathered together her documents and an old diary from the bureau and had stuck everything into the empty grate of her tiled living-room stove.

Early the next morning, all hell seemed to break loose. Orders were shouted, the sounds of army boots echoed from the pavement. A shot was fired and Carmen jumped out of bed. Forgotten were her arthritic joints and she sped to the window. Neighbours, mostly women and children, a very old man and one-legged Herr Brocken on crutches stood in a line facing their houses. More people were being herded into the street as she watched, some still in their night attire, others carrying infants. The soldiers pushed them closer to the walls. A rifle butt was used to speed things up.

More soldiers arrived. They stopped at the door to Carmen's building. Stampeded in. When she heard them on the stairs, she, who was not overtly religious, sank onto her knees and started to pray.

She was manhandled out of her living room and pushed down the stairs. It flashed through Carmen's mind that her friend, Margarete, from the alleyway to the market, had been wrong last night with her assurance that little old ladies with white hair would be spared violence.

Managing to hold on to the banisters, Carmen almost

made it unscathed to ground level. But with another group of soldiers storming up, she had to let go of the handrail. She tripped and stumbled down the last few steps. Her injured leg hurt like mad. All the same, she hobbled out.

For what seemed an eternity, she stood pressed together amidst the others outside. Several times she felt faint. But in order not to pass out and thereby draw attention to herself, she shifted her full weight onto the injured leg. All around her, children were crying, as were some of the women.

From down the street came a piercing scream. Soldiers started yelling at each other.

The shouting grew louder, more excited, uglier.

Then a superior officer sped by in a jeep. Brakes screeched.

Afterwards, the soldiers quietened down. Before long all of them were gone, but not before they had picked up armfuls of booty from the pavement.

Carmen's building had been ransacked, along with the rest. Blankets, quilts, food, dresses, hats, cooking pots, plates, toys, everything imaginable had been dumped at the side of the road. Fragile items were flung with the rest. Everything, that is, except bottles of wine and schnapps. They were carried away like trophies.

Carmen climbed the steps to her flat with some difficulty. A trail of sugar and flour made her fear the worst. On the second floor landing leading to her and her neighbour's flat, discarded clothes littered the area. Carmen's evening gown, wound snakelike around the banister, looked as if it had been through the wringer.

The door to her flat hung ajar. Inside, Carmen picked her way through the mess. Worse than a bungled burglary, she thought. It would take days to sift through it all.

Her glass cabinet was smashed, the bureau had missing legs, the mattress was in shreds, but the skirting board was intact. And, a victorious smile on her lips, she reclaimed the papers and the old diary from the grate of her tiled oven.

Upstairs in the attic things had not gone entirely to plan. The old shoe with Reinhold's booties in it was untouched, but someone must have jumped right onto the pile of spare roof tiles. A number of them were broken and the photo album had been stamped on. But, so Carmen thought, she would be able to salvage about half of the photos. From the miniature painting just a corner of the frame remained. Somebody had liked her picture.

Later that day, sitting amongst the tangle of her belongings, Carmen was moved to chronicle the Russian takeover. Leaving a few pages of her diary blank, she continued where she had left off over twenty years ago.

She promised herself that from now on she would record the events as she experienced them.

Over the years, she did indeed note down her observations. She did so with an eye to Reinhold as her intended reader.

Almost exactly eighteen years later, it was now 1963, Reinhold was sitting in the selfsame chair Carmen had always used when writing. His late mother's diary was resting in his lap. He was about to open it…

Ten days ago, he had finally been given permission by the authorities to travel to Aschersleben. Now that he had prematurely retired, he had been allowed entry into the GDR.

On seeing her son again, Carmen, a frail old lady of

eighty-seven years, had simply been overjoyed. For Reinhold's sake she made herself out to be stronger than she was. Supported by him, they visited places that had long been out of reach for her. And in the evenings they talked. They had years of talking to make up.

She showed him the old photographs, his booties, and told him about the hidden jewellery and where to find it and her diary. "Promise me that you'll read it after I'm gone?" she urged.

"Ach, you've got a few years yet. It's too early to speak of such doom," he said. "But, all right, I promise anyway." He had taken her fragile body into his arms, hugged her until she protested.

But gone she had.

This morning he had found her as if asleep. Her features were relaxed. As he looked down on her, a conviction took hold. "Mother," he said soulfully, "you have died of an excess of happiness."

As Reinhold stood by her bed, he vowed that she was going to be buried as his mother, not Aunty Carmen. She had been the best of mothers...

He was glad he had thanked her for everything she had ever done for him, even though she had cut him short. "Look," she had said last night, "you and I know what we are about." And she had patted his hands.

Now that the day's light had faded, with the standard lamp switched on, Reinhold leaned back in Carmen's writing chair. He blew his nose, then opened his mother's diary and started to read...

# Brunhilde

# Inheritance

It was the morning after Anni's visit and Brunhilde Hopfenstange was storing away the good cognac glasses her husband had requested for last night's little get-together with his 'dear old schoolfriend, Anni'.

'Dear old schoolfriend', Brunhilde could hear her husband's sickly sweet voice all over again. After fifteen years of marriage she knew when he was bullshitting. A look at Anni's face confirmed that she, Anni, was flabbergasted by Peter Hopfenstange's reference to the intimated close friendship.

Having returned the good glasses to their pre-appointed positions inside the display cabinet, Brunhilde slid its door shut. It made a screeching sound. Instantly she was reminded of husband Peter's shrill voice from the night before as he had lamented the country's unification and in particular the Wessis, the West Germans. "We are the poor cousins of the damned Wessis!" he had screeched. "They come here in their Mercedes and expect us to thank them on bended knee…"

He had gone on in the same vein at the top of his voice and she had witnessed him do so. She had also heard him as she listened from behind the door after her rushed exit from the living room. But by then her 'big' husband had become very small under the onslaught of Anni's counter arguments. Brunhilde had been amazed by his turn-about and by his apologetic delivery.

Straightening her broad back – it would have been broad enough for her hubby to hide behind – she turned away from the cabinet. A smile of pleasure settled on Brunhilde's face as she recalled her own quarrel with Peter after Anni's departure.

Because of his run-in with Anni, Brunhilde had expected her husband to be in a filthy mood and was not surprised when he let his spiteful tongue free range. Normally she would have born any accusations with – what anyone else would have termed – saintly patience. But to her own surprise, which was at least equal to his, she had stood her ground.

"I could have done with a bit of wifely support when that woman ranted and raved," he began.

"That woman, I see," Brunhilde mocked; "only a little while ago you called her your dear old friend, remember!"

In the past she used to let his words wash over her, but last night had been different. Maybe it was the sorry figure Peter had cut, or maybe is was Anni's example, whatever it may have been, Brunhilde found the nerve to answer back. "Actually," she said, "Anni is right, the pollution in the GDR was allowed to get out of hand."

Incredulity on his face, Peter Hopfenstange catapulted

himself from his chair and came to a halt right in front of her. "What the…?" was all he managed.

Seeing Peter lost for words, Brunhilde grew bolder. Answering back was a new experience for her. She enjoyed it. With Peter still lost for words, she now said out aloud what, at her most insubordinate, she only would have thought. "But of course," – and she smiled in anticipation of what she was going to say – "nobody dared to object, afraid as we all were, of the Stasi I mean. Though…well, you didn't seem to live in fear… . Let's just say…" Once more, she hesitated before plunging the knife in: "I know things." She looked provocatively into his eyes and nodded when she saw his mouth fall open.

He seemed disorientated. Kept shaking his head. Standing in front of her, his short frame swaying from side to side, he clenched his fists.

Instinctively, Brunhilde also raised her arms. Her jaw jutted forward.

Just for a moment, husband and wife were facing each other like prize-fighters. Until he caved in that is.

"Ach, what do you know!" he said at his most dismissive. He turned and pulled his jacket from the back of his chair. "Anyway, I'm off, need some fresh air."

From then on Brunhilde knew things would never be the same between her and Peter. Her taste of victory, liberation even, was all the greater as she had not experienced anything similar since the age of eighteen, and certainly not since she had become Frau Hopfenstange.

Having finished clearing up after last night, Brunhilde went into the kitchen and made a strong cup of coffee. From the fridge she helped herself to two enormous pieces of cream cheesecake. "To hell with the calories," she muttered and carried the food and drink to the low table in the living room. She sat down in Peter's special armchair. Should he come back home prematurely she would stay put. He would have to ask her nicely to move. She would no longer behave like a frightened rabbit and scarper.

Enjoying her mid-morning break, she asked herself, for the enth time, why Peter had been so accommodating last night, first with Anni and then with her? It had been out of character.

To ingratiate himself with Anni, Brunhilde thought, he had gone as far as claiming that he had opposed the old East German regime. What a turn-about that had been! And it was a lie.

With her, his wife, he had sacrificed a flaming tongue-lashing. Why?

As Brunhilde bit into her second piece of cake, she wondered, could it be that Peter was not as confident as he made out? Did he need her subservience to bolster his ego?

Well, she decided, if he did need her in that way, he was on a losing wicket. Her doormat days were over.

She knew that her friends considered her, if not faint-hearted, a saintly figure. "How do you manage to stay with that bully of a husband?" the closest one had dared ask.

"He's not all bad," she had replied. "He does care, you know." She did not say so, but privately she was embarrassed by her passivity and she suspected that not standing up to Peter had made him more rampant than he otherwise would have been.

After the friend had left, alone with her thoughts, Brunhilde had asked herself whether she would prefer living on her own. But would she really want to return to the small-holding she owned and had run before her marriage?

Until the age of thirty-three, she had scraped a living there, toiling on the land, keeping a couple of goats and chickens. Life had been hard but she had been in charge on the isolated farm.

She remembered that she had hardly seen a soul from one week to the next, had stopped bothering how she looked, had worn the same clothes for weeks and often not washed for days.

One day while digging in the potato field near her cottage, someone, Peter Hopfenstange as she later learned, approached her. Wearing biking gear, his helmet in one hand and a map in the other, he asked for directions to Brandenburg. Being hopelessly lost and because he was polite, Brunhilde invited him into the kitchen where after removing a cackling hen from the table, she drew him a map.

The next time he drove to Brandenburg he made a detour and said hallo.

Soon he called on her regularly. Over coffee and home-baked cake they talked of ordinary things.

He paid her compliments. "You have bottle. You're not one of those shallow girls only interested in clothes and make-up and slimming cures." Another time, he said, blushing, "There's some meat on you. Not like those fashion models, all skin and bones... . Something to get hold of," he added, but immediately apologized for his 'primitive remark'.

Much to her surprise – for she had resigned herself to die an old maid – Brunhilde enjoyed the attention he paid her. For a while she even looked forward to his visits.

But once he started formally to court her, stuffily, and in the way she had read about in romantic novels, bringing her flowers, taking her to the theatre and to meet his mother, she would have preferred not 'to be made a fuss of' as he called it.

She realised then that he loved organising her and knew she ought to put a stop to it. Despite her misgivings, she never said anything, always promising herself to do it next time.

When Peter proposed she was unprepared, even though she should have seen it coming. "You'll make me the happiest man on earth!" he whispered, kneeling in front of her on the kitchen floor. Waiting for her 'yes' – which he somehow seemed to have taken for granted – he got quite agitated. "I can't live without you," he implored her.

She did not know what to say. Eventually she asked for more time to consider his proposal.

Brunhilde was aware that Peter's looks were far removed from those of a romantic hero. His lack of appeal did not trouble her. She could live with his long thin nose, his tadpole-like mouth, the heavy eyebrows, which at times gave his face a menacing expression. After all, she thought, wrongly, as it happened, she was no oil painting.

Apart from his appetite to tell her what to do, his ferret-like zeal in searching out and executing chores was not to her liking either. She would much rather have been left to get on with things, in her own good time.

True, he cared for her. That, she appreciated. But what about love? She concluded that he loved her in his own way. Anyway, what did she know of it! As far as her feelings for him were concerned, she was confused. She did not know what to think and went about in a daze.

So, what was it that tilted the balance for Brunhilde in favour of marriage? Well, it had little if anything to do with Peter, his qualities or lack of them, nor with her feelings. As it happened, it was down to the letter she had received on her eighteenth birthday and the guilt, which had resulted from it.

Sensing that Peter would be badly hurt should she refuse to marry him, instinct – at the time that was what it was, rather than rational argument – forbade her to heap more guilt on herself than she could carry. Making him happy, she thought, would atone for the sins of her father.

Over thirty years had passed since, on her eighteenth birthday, Brunhilde had been given that fateful, life-changing package. And now, after her mid-morning break for coffee and cheesecake, she was holding the very envelope in her hand once more.

Having retrieved it from the bottom of her sewing basket where it – and the enclosed three photographs – had been hidden under balls of knitting wool for fifteen of the thirty years, she carried it with her to the bathroom. She pulled the bolt across the door and sat down on the toilet lid; should Peter come home earlier than expected, she would be undisturbed.

Before opening the envelope, Brunhilde brushed out some creases in the paper. She held the small package up to the light, turned it over several times and then sniffed at it with eyes closed. The strange ritual completed, she gave a heavy sigh. She remembered how excitement had turned into despair as she read the letter for the first time.

On the day Brunhilde had turned eighteen her life had altogether taken a new direction. Fate – or call it what you will – had in the guise of a pointsman thrown a switch and locked her onto a different course. Her slide into masochism had started then, once she learned about a secret of her past, which shocked her into self-loathing.

On the morning of her birthday, by request of her late grandfather's solicitor, Brunhilde had made her way to his office, where she was handed a sealed package. It contained official documents declaring her the legal owner of grandparents Kleeblatt's small-holding as well as a brown envelope, marked: FOR THE EYES OF BRUNHILDE ONLY.

One item inside the envelope was a letter in Georg Kleeblatt's hand. It was dated several weeks before his death.

It read:

Dearest Brunhilde,

My late wife and I have long agonised over whether or not to tell you the truth. Rightly, or wrongly (the future will tell), we decided that you deserve to know.

Even now it is up to you. You may decide NOT to turn this page and read the others I have pinned together. If you tear them up now you will save yourself much heartache. I must warn you that what I have to say will affect your feelings for me and my dear Lisbeth, but more importantly, it will change how you think of yourself. If you go ahead, which I fear – and at the same time hope – you will do, keep one thing uppermost in your mind, overriding everything is the fact that WE LOVE YOU AND HAVE LOVED YOU FROM THE BEGINNING. Remember also that you are the SAME YOU still, after you are in the know.

★★★

Now that you have turned the page you will learn that you are our granddaughter in all but blood. We – I shall continue to refer to ourselves as Granddad and Grandma – were childless.

The picture of our invented, unmarried, daughter, said to have been killed in the Dresden bomb-raid, was a newspaper photo – though it is probably true that your real mother was killed by allied bombs, and I should think that your father is also no longer alive.

Taking you into our home was done from the best of intentions, and from love. We could not have loved a granddaughter by blood better than you.

I wanted to tell you all of this to your face, but didn't have the heart to do so. As I write this, you are still only thirteen years old, too young to be burdened with what follows. Having buried Grandma Lisbeth six months ago (I hope you will continue to think of her, and of me, as your grandparents), I am going to follow her soon. I am seriously ill with cancer and about to die. And you, my little one, will need all your inner resources to cope with the children's home, which I know you will be moved to after my demise.

The truth of the matter is, I found you, sort of sleep-walking, amongst the rubble that was Berlin Spandau in May 1945. We estimated that you were then about three years old. I was alerted by the sounds of pitiful sobbing coming from above the cellar we were living in.

I picked my way up the broken steps of the former storeroom we then called our home and followed my ears. (The basement was all that was left of the once splendid apartment block. After we returned from the shelter one night, we discovered that our flat on the third floor, including belongings, had gone – as if pulverised and blown out of existence. In fact everything in the vicinity above ground had been reduced to piles of debris. It happened during one of the last raids.)

The day you came into our lives, I had been sorting through the handful of cigarette ends, which I had been lucky enough to collect earlier in the morning. I was going to recycle them into roll-ups for Grandma's bartering at her makeshift sales point later.

"See what I've found," I said, half carrying you into the basement. I stood you up on your legs, but they immediately buckled under you.

Despite the mild weather you wore a fur coat. It was much too large, and consequently, once we managed to stand you upright, you kept stepping on its hem.

But you screamed as soon as we tried to take the coat off.

Grandma comforted you and asked for your name. You gave no answer. Oblivious of your surroundings, you called for your mother. Grandma offered you one of her special titbits – a biscuit baked with real butter, but you refused it. Eventually you could not keep your eyes open and we bedded you down on a spare bench.

All through the next day, the little one, as we called you, didn't speak. You just stared in front of you, seemed to have lost your tongue. Traumatised, we thought; you didn't look retarded.

Your coat – even though it was covered in dust, the torn velvety skirt and the woollen jumper you wore all spoke of quality. We assumed some well-to-do family had lost you.

I searched for several weeks, must have stopped to talk to hundreds of people in my attempt to find out who was missing a child. I checked the missing-person notices.

In the meantime a change had come over you. You babbled away happily and no longer called for your mother. We started to call you 'Engelchen', on account of your silky blond hair and blue eyes.

Gradually, you became a permanent fixture; your sweet nature lightened our hardships. To my shame, I have to confess that I stopped inquiring about missing children, for fear that you might be taken from us.

This fear lay at the heart of our decision to move to a small farm outside Brandenburg to help

Grandma Lisbeth's sister with the running of it.

Before the onset of winter Grandma decided that your fur coat needed repairing. As Grandma's fingers searched for anything torn, she thought she could feel something hard inside the hem. As it needed sewing anyway, she cut through the worn manual stitching and extracted what at first she took to be a small sewing kit. But instead of the expected needles and thread it contained three small photographs, and wrapped up in a piece of velvet cloth she discovered five sparkling, finely cut diamonds the size of a pea down to a grain of rice.

The first of the photos showed a smiling, Aryan-looking SS Officer standing in front of a high, closed metal gate. 'ARBEIT MACHT FREI' said the inscription over the top. The same uniformed man was depicted in the second photo, he was part of a group saluting Hitler's image on the occasion of some sort of celebration. The third photo showed the man again, but this time he was in civilian clothes holding hands with a pretty young woman and a little girl. All three of the people had been photographed standing in front of a Christmas tree, facing the camera. On the back of this photo, it said: Herman, Hildegard and little Brunhilde, taken at home, Christmas Eve 1944, on Brunhilde's second birthday.

"So, Brunhilde is the little one's name," Grandma said at last.

I just nodded. I was shocked. Don't forget, I narrowly

missed being sent to one of those concentration camps. "Why would this woman," I eventually said, "why would this Hildegard want to save her husband's SS pictures, if she wasn't a sympathiser?" I felt angry, but sad as well. "To save the family photo and the precious stones made sense, but not..."

Grandma kept shaking her head. "The mother must have realised the war was lost and that these photos could incriminate the child."

We talked about what might have happened to your mother and supposed that she had been killed. Finally, your grandma summed up the situation, "It seems we have taken the child of a KZ-guard to our hearts."

"Look," I said, "none of this is the little one's fault." With Grandma nodding agreement, I proposed to keep the photos and diamonds secret; for the time being, anyway. "We will tell Brunhilde – that's what we call her from now on – when she's ready for it."

I have to stop now, getting emotional. I just wished...

With all my, and Grandma's, love.

Georg Kleeblatt's shaky signature followed.

PS I shall not be alive when you reach the age of

majority, as I will soon join Grandma Kleeblatt. You are only thirteen years old and I am therefore handing the three photos, the five diamonds and this letter for safe-keeping to my trusted solicitor and friend. He will contact you when the time comes. I hope you will accept the small-holding as your own. With the other things you must do as you see fit. I am so sorry not to be there on your 18th., to stand by you.

One final thing: FORGIVE YOURSELF! YOU ARE NOT RESPONSIBLE FOR WHAT YOUR FATHER DID!

Brunhilde had finished re-reading Granddad's letter, and the yellowing pages had slipped onto her lap. Tears were running down her cheeks, with the odd one dropping onto the dry-as-dust paper, making a slight plopping noise. She did not hear it. Cherished images from the past were floating by. Pictures of her grandparents, the farm, harvest time… . White-bearded Granddad paused in front of her. With index finger raised, he implored her, "Forgive yourself!" thereby repeating what she had just read.

Feeling herself slipping sideways, Brunhilde steadied herself. Bending forward, she screwed up her eyes, in the way she did when she was concentrating hard.

Eventually, her chin jutted forward. She had made up her mind.

For a start, she thought, Granddad would be proud of her. His wish that she put her guilt into perspective was coming true.

Before the day was out she was going to talk to Peter, really talk.

She was going to let him read the letter – she was sure

Granddad would not have minded – and she would try to make her husband understand how she had been affected by the revelations all those years ago, and nearer the present...

She had only just left the children's home when Granddad's letter had come to her. It was after she and the others had been shown pictures of gas chambers, ovens, of piles of dead bodies, heaps of hair, of skeletal survivors of concentration camps. It had been the stuff of nightmares. So, when she learned of her father's involvement in Hitler's barbarity – well, at least of his guilt by association – she was devastated. There was nobody she could talk to, to lighten the burden. In any case, she would have been too ashamed to admit that she was and felt tainted. How could she have laughed, danced, flirted like other girls? The knowledge of where she descended from made her feel an outcast.

As Brunhilde sat on the toilet seat in the bathroom of her and husband Peter's comfortable home, she wondered whether he would twig about certain motives on her part...

She planned to bring the talk round to the topic of the fall of the Wall, and to Anni's visit. Brunhilde suspected, had the Wall not fallen, she might have gone on fooling herself into believing that she and Peter lived the life of an ordinary couple. She also believed that Anni's visit had been the final nail in the coffin of illusory contentment.

Post-1989, Brunhilde had become aware of evils perpetrated by the successors of the Nazi secret police. It disturbed her that the unmasked Stasis rarely blamed themselves, claiming to have followed orders and to have acted in good faith.

Yet, she had taken guilt on board! For the sins of her father. But compared with the Stasi-perpetrators, she was a victim. Was she not?

During their talk to come, Brunhilde also hoped that Peter would confide his own transgressions. Despite her taunt last night, she did not know much about his murkier activities, though she had benefited. Colleagues, Party members, others she did not know used to turn up at the house, usually after work and Peter talked with them behind closed doors. Crates of wine, building material and other scarce items were soon, as if by coincidence, delivered under cover of darkness. Anyway, Peter's prosperity in the old GDR seemed suspicious; as did the ease with which he had acquired Wartburg cars. And then there was the house…

One thing Brunhilde was sure of: her conversation with Peter would make or break their marriage.

Downstairs a key was being turned in the front door, followed by Peter's familiar steps. "Liebling, are you there?" he called.

He hasn't called me that since we were newly-weds, she thought, and stood up. She gathered the pages of Granddad's letter and the photos of her father together.

Fleetingly, she thought of the five diamonds hidden inside her little girl's coat hem. Would Peter have been tempted…? Maybe it was just as well that she had donated the stones to her children's home, long ago, anonymously.

## Ina & Theo

## Green-eyed Monster

He's not kept his promise, Ina thought. Feeling annoyed with her husband, Theo, she was regarding him with knitted brows. The longer she watched him, the angrier she grew.

Theo was standing at the other end of Eduard's living room; he held a half-bottle of whisky in one hand and a full glass in the other. A telltale flush of red had settled over his cheeks and he was wiping his sweaty forehead.

Warning bells rang in Ina's head, making her feel apprehensive. Once fully inebriated her husband was capable of behaving irrationally. She remembered how only last week he had to be restrained at their local…all because a fellow regular had paid her a compliment.

After she and Theo had first arrived to celebrate Eduard's successful one-man exhibition in far-off Munich she had reminded Theo that this evening it was his turn to stay sober and that at the end of the party he was to drive them both home.

"Look," Ina said, after she had crossed the floor and stood before him – with his six-foot-three he was towering above her – "you agreed it was mineral water for you. So, what's this you're drinking?" She tapped her finger against his glass.

"That soft drink idea was yours," Theo said, aggrieved. "I didn't have a say, did I?" He gave her a strained smile before draining his glass. "Anyway, stop nagging and leave me alone. I need something to make this party tolerable for me," he huffed. "What with Eduard flouncing about and dancing attention to that Karin woman."

Ina gave him a dirty look. "Karin woman, I see. Watch it!" She jabbed a manicured finger at his chest. "You do know that you're talking about a very good friend of mine. What has she done to you, hmm?" She gave another, harder, jab and exhaled loudly. That's a new one on me, she thought, making Karin the scapegoat for the green-eyed monster.

"Come on, out with it," she snapped. "Admit what you're really sore about," and reducing the volume of her voice to a whisper, she said, "I noticed you staring while Eduard chatted to me."

"If you say so," Theo smirked, rather meanly.

"I see, pretending to be blasé." Ina knew better; Theo was miffed all right, even though the sole reference he had ever made to Eduard's 'tittle-tattle' – and drink had been talking then – was: "What's this puny artist fellow got that I haven't?"

"D'you know what?" Ina said, and this time she prodded her husband none too gently with her elbow. "I would enjoy more gallantry on your part, 'dancing attention' as you put it I suppose. You haven't said a word to me all evening."

As she straightened up to her full five foot two inches

in high heels, she sighed, then said under her breath, "Am I meant to be grateful that you didn't accuse Eduard of chatting me up? Is that it?"

Ina paused, but there was no reply.

"Anyway," she continued, glaring at Theo, "you'll do well to remember that there's nothing between Eduard and me," and she threw her head back with a flourish.

"As if I've ever mentioned any hanky-panky," came Theo's sharp reproof.

But before Ina could step away to rejoin the party, his sour mood suddenly lifted. In buddy-like manner he drew her close and whispered in her ear, "We'd be better off at home." Taking hold of her arm, he guided her away from the proximity of other party guests as not to be overheard. "Why don't we make an excuse and slip away, sweetheart?" he said. "What do you say, hmm? Let's go. It's a boring party." He smiled, pursed his lips and blew her a kiss. "I'll phone for a taxi."

"Don't you dare!" Ina stamped her foot. She no longer minded who could hear. Theo's overture and his hush-hush manner had repelled her as much as the suggested premature departure itself. As far as she was concerned the party was only just warming up.

She took the whisky bottle and the glass out of his hands and stood the censored items on the sideboard. "You'll be better off with some strong black coffee." She nudged him towards the kitchen and then walked away.

Realising that Karin was looking at her from across the room, Ina remembered how only days ago, during their lunch break in the hospital staff canteen, Karin had asked, "Why doesn't Theo like me?" And then she had gone on to explain that it was just a feeling she had, and that she could not really put her finger on it.

Ina had pooh-poohed her friend, saying, "Nonsense, you're mistaken, you're imagining it." But now, here in Eduard's living room, Ina was no longer sure that it was nothing. Her husband had uttered her friend's name with unseemly venom.

As she was giving a cordial wave back to Karin, Ina was struck by her friend's radiance. She certainly doesn't look as if she's worrying about Eduard's faithfulness. My husband must be goggle-eyed if he reads serious intent into Eduard's light-hearted chat-up lines.

Going over to the drink trolley Ina helped herself to a glass of Gewürztaminer. She was not sacrificing her favourite wine just because Theo had not abstained. They would have to take a taxi home. But later, and not before the evening was out.

Ina took a good swig from her glass. She was determined to enjoy herself despite her wet-blanket husband.

It was there and then that she decided she would have that heart-to-heart with Karin. Her friend and colleague had twenty years on her. Yes, Ina thought, Karin knows a thing or two about life, and it won't be that hard to open up to her. She's got the sort of lived-in face that inspires confidences.

Lately, in quiet moments, Ina had admitted to herself that her marriage was in trouble. It was not so much that Theo had changed, she had. And he did not like it.

She was no longer in awe of her fifteen-year-older husband. Aged nineteen, and an immature student, she had agreed to get married – much too young, as she now thought.

Looking back, she had enjoyed Theo's dominance. His

possessiveness had flattered her, and the few misgivings she did have on that score were soon counterbalanced by his charming attentiveness. He seemed to read her every wish and was at her beck and call. Was it surprising that she considered herself superior to other women whose husbands seemed less worshipful of their wives? Wasn't Theo's constant devotion proof of his ardent love? Having been adopted at the age of eight by a well-meaning but non-demonstrative professional couple she lapped up his affectionate care.

It was when – after graduating and taking up a responsible appointment as theatre anaesthetist – she started to have an outside life of her own and make new friends that her husband grew resentful of the changed situation. Theo did not forbid her anything, but he left her in no doubt whenever he was not pleased about her conduct. She soon learned to recognise a glum expression and petulant gestures as the first signs of disapproval, and, if not heeded, a cantankerous mood would take hold of him. And because she did not like strained atmospheres at home, and because she needed her free time to relax she had tended to give in. After all, didn't he deserve consideration? Furthermore, she was grateful to him for having supported her financially – as well as emotionally – throughout her student days.

But in more recent days, Ina had become less tolerant of her husband's sulking. Consequently, they were frequently at odds with one another.

For instance, today had not started well. Right from the morning Theo had tried to persuade Ina not to go to Eduard's and Karin's party. But she had stood her ground. Why should she forego her pleasures just because her husband felt threatened by Eduard? There was no reason at all for Theo to worry. A bit of innocent flirting never did anybody any harm. She was not his property. "If you don't want to come, fine, I'll go on my own," she had finally said.

※

A catchy tune from Eduard's stereo system intruded into Ina's pondering. Several couples started dancing.

Now, Ina thought, is not the time for brooding. She liked nothing better than a good party; and Eduard's gathering of friends was turning into just one of those.

Soon she was the darling of her dancing partners, and in between gliding across the floor, there was delicious gossiping – all in good humour.

Getting her breath back after the latest rumba and seeing the drink trolley parked forlornly in one corner, she got hold of it and pushed it around the room, offering the stacked-up goodies.

She caught Eduard's eye and he directed her to, in his words, 'still serious-looking guests'.

"Let's liven things up," he said, once he was standing next to her. And with a wink and a nudge he volunteered her to perform the Charleston.

Ina, dressed in white silk pantaloons and flowery chiffon blouse, looked the part. The only thing missing was one of those 1920s' long cigarette holders. The music ringing out seemed to electrify her trim figure. Her knife-edged auburn pageboy haircut framed her elfin face with its sparkly blue eyes and undulated as she showed off her sidekicks.

Everybody was looking at the routine. Standing at the side of the dance floor, Theo too was watching, though his face was dark as thunderclouds. Spoilsport, Ina thought, catching a glimpse of him. As she whirled past, she also thought she could see a bottle and a drink in his hands. She could almost hear him reproach her, accusing her of making a spectacle of herself and letting the side down. But being buoyed up by the goodwill all around and riding the crest of the wave, she was past caring.

Eventually Ina found herself dancing with Eduard. As they moved effortlessly across the floor, she rested her head against his shoulder and he bent down and brushed her hair with his lips.

The sound of crashing glass made her open her eyes. The sorry sight offering itself was of dishevelled Theo – he was no longer wearing his pullover and one of his shirt-tails had worked itself loose. His face was dripping sweat as he stood, uncomprehending, over the splintered remains of his drink.

When Karin approached with brush and pan in hand, Ina hustled her husband to the kitchen. "Now," she commanded, "you'll have that black coffee."

On the way to the kitchen, Theo knocked the receiver off the cradle and started to dial. "Taxi," he pleaded.

Ina did not relent and fought with him for possession of the telephone. The tussle lasted until she jabbed his toes with her stiletto heel.

The dancing had finished some time earlier and the party was quietening down. Some of the guests had already left. Those remaining were sitting in small groups and talking – apart from the few who had wandered back to the kitchen to help themselves to more food.

Eduard and Karin were talking with Anni and another guest, Axel, when Ina breezed in. With a sigh she allowed herself to collapse onto the upturned carpet and crawled to where Eduard was sitting, settling her back against his knees.

"Right!" Theo snarled from the other side of the room. He scrambled to his feet, towering above everyone. "We're going. I'm getting a taxi."

Ina sat up. "I'll go when I'm good and ready."

Everyone stopped talking.

"It's early yet, Theo, come and sit down," said Axel, pointing to a chair.

"Yes, cool it, man." Eduard spoke gaily, getting up from his seat. With his hand outstretched, he took a step towards Theo.

Brushing Eduard's hand aside, Theo stomped up to his wife. "We're going! Now!"

Before Ina had time to say anything, Eduard placed himself in front of her. "Come on, Theo, there's no need for that." His voice was calm.

"Don't tell me how to speak to my wife!" Theo exploded. "I don't tell you how to treat your fucking Stasi-bitch!"

Eduard looked stunned, he kept shaking his head. His fingers formed into a fist. He looked at it abstractedly as though it did not belong to him. Then, suddenly, he threw himself forward…

After Eduard had delivered his punch, Theo staggered and stumbled backwards, his whole body shuddered as it struck the wall behind him. One of Eduard's glazed pastels crunched under the force of the impact. Pieces of glass fell out of the frame as his crumpling figure slid down the wall, dragging the picture with him.

Karin took charge then. "Stop it! Both of you!" she shouted. "Stop behaving like bloody imbeciles!"

Eduard, still with that look of incredulity on his face, stepped aside.

But Karin was not yet finished with Theo. Kicking the leg of the chair he had been helped into, she told him,

"We might as well settle this right here, and sod your bleeding back! I've never had anything to do with the STASI." Shoving her face close to his, she accused him, "You know nothing! You weren't even there. You were safe in the West. We were living with those damned creeps."

Theo cringed under Karin's onslaught, yet she went on… . Finally, a sneer spread across her face and looking first at Eduard and then at Ina, she said over her shoulder, "Another thing, Theo—" she made the name sound like a dirty word "—Eduard and Ina aren't having an affair. You've been getting up my nose over that."

By the time Karin had moved away from Theo he looked very small. He rubbed his chest and moaned while Ina rolled up his torn shirt and put it in her handbag. "Your pullover will have to do until we get home," she said.

She was feeling guilty for having contributed to Theo's hateful outburst and now assumed the role of dutiful wife. Taking her hosts aside, she apologised for her part in the whole sorry incident.

Karin reassured her, "Don't worry, I won't let it spoil our friendship."

When the taxi arrived, Ina said a hasty goodbye, but Theo ignored everyone present.

The next morning, Sunday, Ina got up late. Theo who last night had been banned to the spare room was nowhere to be seen.

"You can't evade talking to me," she said through the door. "Remember what we agreed?" But there was no answer.

Two hours later he still had not surfaced and she began

to feel worried. What if he'd overdosed? He took the occasional sleeping tablet when he felt stressed.

A look inside the bathroom cabinet established that the tablets were still there. Was she being melodramatic?

When she eventually entered the room, after first ridiculing herself for imagining him hanging from the light fitting, there was no sign of him. He had tidied the bed, even shifted the pile of books from the floor to the shelf – something she had been meaning to do for at least a week. Feeling upbraided, she swore, "Damn your orderliness!"

She went on to search the room, the rest of their flat, for a note, for anything to explain his absence, but found nothing. Had she overestimated her importance to him?

Anyway, if she was to avoid driving in the dark on this freezing January afternoon, to get to the hotel near the hospital, she had to make haste. It was not how she had envisaged leaving; she had wanted to explain to Theo why, after much heart searching, she had decided on a separation.

After packing a few essentials she took the lift to the underground car park and walked up to her yellow VW Beetle. Theo's space next to hers was glaringly unoccupied. So, that's what he's done, he's gone for a long drive, somewhere…but couldn't spare the time for a note.

And then, as she edged out of the garage, Theo showed up on his way in. He wound his window down and, gesticulating madly, he indicated to her to stop.

Just for a moment she hesitated. But his wild eyes and agitated demeanour put her off talking to him. Had he noticed the two suitcases next to her, she wondered, and shaking her head, she drove on.

Soon enough he would find the message she had scrawled with lipstick over the bathroom mirror. And he could always contact her at work.

Four days later Ina returned to the flat, together with Karin who had insisted on coming along. "You can't be sure what mood he'll be in," Karin had argued. "Besides, you need help with carting your stuff."

Ina unlocked the door without difficulty. She could see the lights on in the corridor and kitchen where some broken plates littered the floor. "Where are you, Theo?" she called. His car had been parked in its allotted space.

Everything remained dead quiet. Where could he be…?

"Let's make a start," Karin suggested, and walked towards the kitchen.

Ina headed for the bathroom. She wanted to see if her message on the mirror was still there.

It was. What was more, Theo had added to it. Below her words:

"I CAN NO LONGER LIVE WITH YOU. I AM LEAVING," Theo had written, with lipstick also:

"AND I WON'T LIVE WITHOUT YOU!!"

As Ina looked at the red letters, which seemed to drip blood, she heard a horrified scream.

When Karin stumbled through the door, looking as white as a ghost, Ina knew…

"You don't want to see…" Karin whispered, holding Ina tight. "Theo is beyond help…hanging…"

Once Ina's sobbing eased, she kept repeating, "If only I'd stopped the car and talked to him… . He might still be alive…"

# *Amadeus*

# *Repercussions*

Amadeus was making his way along the esplanade in Weimar. The lusty breeze frolicked with his longish light-brown hair as if it were an Afghan hound's. He walked with a spring in his step but stopped – as he always used to do in the days he lived in the town – outside the Schiller House, to look up at the first-floor windows. He imagined the great man, sitting bent over at his desk, working. What gems of thought had come to life on the page! Did Goethe visit there for writerly discussions? During Schiller's time here from 1802 to 1805 and through Goethe's influence this town became the centre of German classicism.

Amadeus had moved away from Weimar last year, in 1992 – to take up his new post and not from any desire for greener pastures – and welcomed every opportunity to come back to his favourite place. To celebrate the birthday of his cousin, Angelika, was reason enough for a short pilgrimage, and hence he had chosen to take a day off from his orchestral duties in Berlin.

Dressed in a pinstripe suit with ruche shirt for the sake of his cousin, an old-maidish but likeable snob, who collected minor – he thought in his case very minor – celebrities, Amadeus was about to walk on. But before doing so his eyes happened to glance over to the nearby fountain. A sweeper standing in front of it was leaning on his broom, seemingly taking a breather from work and, at his leisure, he was looking around and observing the people go by.

*God!* Amadeus thought, *that brings back memories; this chap's doing what I used to do when I had his job.*

The instant he pictured himself sweeping, Amadeus frowned, but then the next moment his features brightened again. *It wasn't all bad*, he said to himself. *Anyway, that was what I used to tell family and friends when they inquired and expressed their regrets to see me working as a menial.*

He remembered, he had almost convinced himself that he did not mind the job – not that he could have done anything to change the situation he found himself in. Now, in retrospect he was quite sure that his positive attitude had prevented him from falling into despair.

The sweeper at the fountain was still taking things easy. He noticed Amadeus looking at him and raised his cap.

Amadeus responded by lifting the instrument case with his flute, and by giving a friendly nod. *Yes*, he thought, redolent of days past, *being a sweeper had its compensations. Definitely. And my successor oozes humour. He's bound to appreciate the freedom to think that goes with the job.*

As Amadeus turned and went on his way, a little smile spread over his face. *Wouldn't you know, nostalgia with its rose-coloured paint! Stay here much longer and I'll ask for my old job back.* He pulled a face. *Come now!*

But walking on to Angelika's, other memories came to his mind. The other side of the coin, he thought. There had been times when he'd had to deal with objectionable characters during a shift. Pictures rose up in his mind...

The trouble with Dirty-jeans and Black-leather attacking Curly-head had not been an isolated one. No reason to assume that the situation concerning hooligans had recently improved. Ever since the Wall had come down the iron hand of the GDR State no longer held the troublemakers in check. And there aren't too many Victors about to give assistance to a sweeper!

Amadeus pictured the powerfully built Englishman commanding Dirty-jeans to let go of Curly-head. Just for a moment, Dirty-jeans had loosened his grip, but when he thrust his hand into Curly's jacket pocket to get hold of the latter's car keys, Victor's arm shot out. He grabbed the skinhead by the front of his orange shirt – there was a ripping sound as he heaved the youth off the ground; with his free hand he screwed Dirty-jeans' right ear, kneeing him in the groin as he did so, then shoving him aside. The second skinhead, Black-leather then came forward. He looked at Victor, wondering if he could take him. Victor was taller, sturdy, and he was serious. Scuffing one boot against the pavement, Black-leather glanced from Victor to him, Amadeus, holding his broom in a deliberately threatening way. "Ach," grunted the skinhead. With a dismissive gesture of his hand he tried to give the impression that he could not be bothered. He went over to Dirty-jeans and pulled him to his feet. Swearing and spitting on the ground, they made their exit – Dirty-jeans hobbling away.

After the incident with the skinheads, which, with Victor's help, had ended in their defeat and ignoble retreat, and after silk-suited Curly-head's deferential expression of gratitude for his rescue, Amadeus and Victor had stayed on the esplanade, talked and exchanged addresses. That had been way back in August 1991.

※

As Amadeus pressed the bell at Angelika's house, he felt a sudden pang of guilt. He still had not answered Victor's letter, written over half a year ago at Christmas. True, he had sent a Christmas greeting card to England, but he had not honoured the promise he had made in the PS to write a long reply, so far – despite his firm belief that Victor would love to read what he, Amadeus, had to tell.

The outstanding letter had actually become more urgent since part of the information Amadeus planned to convey concerned something deplorable, but also rather intriguing. It had to do with machination and subterfuge, which he himself had only recently learned about. He could telephone, of course, in fact had done so a couple of times since Christmas, but he felt the nature of the news was rather complex and needed exposition.

How fortuitous to have met Victor, Amadeus thought, the least he could do was to keep up the correspondence. He considered Victor his soul-mate. All the more so, since he too had experienced life under repression while teaching English in pre-Tiananmen China.

Amadeus was well aware that without his friend's continuous encouragement to return to his calling he might still be sweeping the roads today.

Victor practically forced him to submit the composition "Blue" which won Amadeus a first prize. On the strength of that win he was employed again as a flautist after years of absence from professional music making.

As always when Amadeus remembered their first meeting he was amazed how easily he had opened up to Victor. On that warm sunny August afternoon, intimate details of his life had rolled off his tongue as if he were talking to a lifelong friend.

"Used to be a flautist, professional, long time ago," Amadeus had confided. Having decided to talk, chunks of words spewed forth like lava: "Fell out of favour, critical of the party, see." Gazing dreamily at Victor, he had added, "But I've started playing again, just for fun."

Encouraged by Victor's interest, Amadeus spoke candidly of his life as a musician and how it had come to an abrupt end when he was sacked from his post. He expressed his suspicion that it was probably an unguarded comment, overheard and reported by someone, which had changed everything for him.

As Amadeus eventually admitted, he had been unhappy and depressed, but he had not allowed his demotion in 1985 to crush him. After '89, overcoming his nerves at merely taking a flute in his hand, he had actually bought one, and had dared to play it, privately at first, just for fun. At the time of meeting Victor, he had started, tentatively, to play for a public again.

It had taken Amadeus ages to regain his former standard of play and still he had lacked the confidence to apply for professional work. Entering for the prize and winning had made all the difference…

Amadeus was still waiting for Angelika to open the door. He knew she hated to be hurried, so he stood patiently on her step for a while longer.

In his mind, he started to compose the belated letter

to Victor. The delay, Amadeus would explain, was due to his lengthy efforts to get to read his Stasi-file. Yes, little ol' me – he was to say – had been considered important enough to be reported on.

There were stacks of pages of their surveillance stuff. Victor, too, he thought, would laugh out aloud when learning how the whole thing started.

At the root of Amadeus's Stasi-trouble, way back in 1983 had been – so it transpired – his Irish wolfhound-come-lurcher-come-bearded-collie, Barney. He was the *baddy* who first fell foul of these horrid people.

Being a five-year-old rescue dog without known history, Barney was wayward and right from the beginning difficult to control. But he was a real character, and no way was he going back to the dog sanctuary. At home he was the softest, most tender, lovable friend imaginable. He was the cutest littlest wolfhound anyone ever saw. But there was a down side: Barney hated visitors, most other dogs, and he was overprotective. Out walking with his boss, he would bark and lurch at anyone or anything that came too close. He particularly hated bikes, men and furniture removal vans.

Somehow, dog and keeper managed without getting into scrapes – until, apparently, a fellow player of Amadeus in the orchestra moved house and settled very near to the latter's place. Benjamin Gerstenkorn was the name of the new neighbour.

Walking Barney, Amadeus had made it a rule not to stop on the way and attempt to chat with friends, family, neighbours, anyone. However, on the day in question, Barney seemed unusually peaceable and hence made it possible for Amadeus to exchange a few words with Benjamin. "Barney is friendly today," he remarked.

Maybe it was hearing his name spoken by a stranger? Anyway – whatever it was - something surely prompted Barney to start his usual clamour.

Partly in exasperation, partly in disappointment at Barney's renewed belligerence, Amadeus shouted, "Why don't you shut your mouth!" Then, sighing, he had pulled the dog away, muttering, "Come on, let's go."

Amadeus forgot about the incident soon enough. But not Benjamin. Oh, no! In his record of it, he attributed sinister motives to Amadeus, accusing him of antagonism. The angry shout was said to have been merely a cover to vent his hostility towards him, Benjamin, the operative and representative of the authorities. Why else – so Benjamin argued – had Amadeus not addressed the dog by name?

Reading his file in the privacy of an office cubicle, Amadeus had been incredulous. The outlandish argument made him shake his head. For God's sake, it was a clear-cut case! The circumstances were such that he needn't have bent down to holler into the dog's ear or stare him into the eyes to address him. At any rate, he didn't know then that Benjamin was one of *them*; and Amadeus had had no idea just how far the paranoia of the operatives spanned, that they saw enemies everywhere.

But once Amadeus had been brought to the attention of Benjamin's superiors, that was, in their bizarre thinking, reason enough for surveillance. From then on, Benjamin filed regular reports and became Amadeus's special watcher. Everything went into the reports, remarks to do with shortages, as well as totally non-political derogatory snipes at fellow musicians. Then, in 1985, Amadeus had made an inflammatory anti-government comment. Anyway, it was thought to be serious enough to warrant expulsion from the orchestra.

Amadeus pressed Angelika's bell for the second time. He looked at his watch. Yes, he was on time. Where was she?

After a moment or two there was a crackle on the intercom: "Angelique de Blanc's residence," whispered a delicate voice.

*I see*, he thought and grimaced, *Madame de Blanc, I understand. Angelika Weiss's too pedestrian for you. So, I better not fall foul of my cousin's latest affectation. Right!* Aloud he said, "Amadeus Mozart for Angelique de Blanc."

"My dear Amadeus, do come in," a robust lady in her fifties, belying her frail little voice, pulled him indoors. They looked at each other and burst out laughing. "Madame de Blanc is just for today," she winked.

"Why not indeed," Amadeus smiled. "After all it's your fif—" he started to say fifty-second but corrected himself "—it's your birthday."

Angelika was such fun to be with and he easily forgave her the putting on of airs. It was only a game to her, no harm in that. Despite being snobbish she had never cut him dead in the days he swept the roads.

"I'm glad you've come to help with the food," Angelika said. "The others won't be here for at least an hour." She fluttered her eyelids. "You know, you're renowned for your salads, and you arrange them so artistically." She took his hand, "Come on, let's go. All the bits and pieces await you on the kitchen table."

But before she allowed the apron-attired eager Amadeus loose on the ingredients, she poured out a couple of glasses of champagne.

Setting his emptied glass down on the dresser, Amadeus asked, "Who are these important guests you have insisted on keeping secret from me? You didn't tell Auntie Rosa either. I got the impression over lunch with her that she's a teeny bit hurt about that."

Ignoring Amadeus's reproach, Angelika straightened up to full height. "Well," she said, her smile full of promise, "there's Marcel, I mean Marc; he's going to read from his recently published volume of poems. One of them he dedicated to me." She nodded proudly and seemed to grow even taller. "Then there's Charlotte with her quirky biography of Schiller. I've read it, it's bound to take off. Anton, you know, the true bohemian with his impressive profile. He will give a recital on my Bechstein. And, of course, not forgetting you with your prize-winning composition, 'Blue'." She paused for breath and drew him to her black lace-swathed bosom. "I can't wait for the evening to begin." Having released Amadeus, she whispered, "And, on top of everything else—" She paused again, this time for effect, her lips parted and the top of her pink tongue showed. "Yes, on top of everything else, you'll never guess, I've invited your dear old friend and colleague, from the old days…" She hesitated, waiting for a flicker of recognition.

There was none.

"Well," she continued, ever so slightly peeved, "I've invited Benjamin Gerstenkorn," and more forcefully, she added, "for you specially." The emphatic 'There!' remained unsaid, though it hung in the air.

Amadeus, who had in the meantime started to cut the green peppers for the mixed salad, grew pale. He let go of the knife. It slithered off the cutting board and lodged in the soft leather of his shoe.

"Outch!" he yelled, before quickly bending down to retrieve the knife. "It's okay," he reassured Angelika, wiggling his toes inside the shoe. "No harm done."

To draw the attention away and to stop her from asking awkward questions, he conveniently remembered something. Slapping his forehead, he piped, "How could I have forgotten your present? Just one teeny-weeny moment."

He rushed from the kitchen, away from Angelika's scrutiny. He urgently needed to compose himself. His cousin was not to know that Benjamin Gerstenkorn was the last person on earth Amadeus would want to mix with socially. Nevertheless, he had to play along or risk disrupting Angelika's precious birthday party. He would have to pretend to be pleased to see his former fellow orchestral player from the 'eighties. Yes, he told himself, that was what he had to do.

He returned with a gift-wrapped bottle of French perfume.

"Oh, how did you know!" Angelika breathed on unwrapping the present.

❦

Marc had finished reading from his slim volume of poetry. His poetry was matched by the power of his performance and from around the room lavish applause was forthcoming. Angelika seemed enthralled. But she sobered enough to make sure that Marc's dedication of the last poem to her did not go unnoticed.

Amadeus thought, Marc had made fun in it of his cousin by not too subtly caricaturing her. But since she was unaware of the flaws in her character, she did not see it that way. Luckily for Marc.

"Impressive style, don't you think?" she said, having caught up with Amadeus in the kitchen. But she did not wait for his reply. Instead, she commented on BG, Benjamin Gerstenkorn's lateness, interpreting it as a slight on her illustrious gathering. "He seemed overjoyed to accept my invite," she said. "He assured me that he would cancel all appointments to be here on time."

Angelika leaned closer: "And so he might! What other appointments?" she snickered. "Who else of my standing would invite a lowly garden-centre assistant? Invitations to my dos don't grow on trees. You agree?"

BG working in a garden centre! His turn for demotion? Enjoying a touch of Schadenfreude, but not wanting to show it, Amadeus chewed his bottom lip. And, despite Angelika pushing for an answer, he kept quiet.

Somewhat offended, Angelika turned away and left Amadeus standing. His mind was ticking over: *if BG suspects that I know about his unsavoury activities then he's bound to steer clear of the party. But, what if Angelika didn't tell him that I was coming? She didn't tell me about his invitation until the last moment…*

Half an hour passed and BG still had not arrived.

"Do you see much of Benjamin these days?" Amadeus said to Anton, casually, when they, literally, bumped into each other whilst refilling their glasses. "I take it the two of you still belong to the local amateur dramatics group?"

"No, we don't," Anton said, uncharacteristically abrupt. He shook himself as if he had swallowed a spider.

Amadeus's inquiry had been designed to test the water. Was he to assume that Anton, too, knew Benjamin's secret? After all, Anton, if anyone, would be the one in the know. He and Benjamin had been the best of friends.

Anyway, the unexpected question had agitated Anton. He, who was most articulate, started to stammer. Finally he got a grip on himself, "Hear no evil, see no evil," he said, and placed his index finger against his lips. "It's all in the past. I don't hold any grudges."

It was loaded language. And while Amadeus was still thinking about Anton's reply, the latter looked around before whispering, "BG did the dirty on me. He was a despicable informer."

"Yes, I know," Amadeus said.

Anton did not seem the least surprised.

※

Two hours later, the artistic offerings of Angelika's guests were coming to an end. Charlotte had read from her Schiller biography, Anton had given his recital on the Bechstein, and Amadeus was playing the final notes of 'Blue' when the bell shrilled. It was Benjamin.

His oil-smeered hands testified to his breakdown on the road. "I had no way to let you know," he said, apologising to Angelika. "My motorbike has never let me down before."

It was fortunate that the party guests crowded around the latecomer and thus were spared the look of loathing in Amadeus's eyes.

Despite his revulsion at the sight of Benjamin, Amadeus kept looking at him, as if fascinated. Standing steps away from him, Amadeus compared the remembered image of his former colleague with the bedraggled figure in front of him. Even without the dirt and oil stains on his sweaty face, he was a mere shadow of his old, audacious self. He had aged beyond his years and looked haggard, and he studiously avoided eye contact; Amadeus was sure of it because he had seen Benjamin's mouth twitch on recognising him.

*Frightened Benjamin is shitting himself*, Amadeus thought. But stirrings of pity were short-lived when he recalled the damage that man had done to him. Being forced to sweep roads was not all of it…out of the recesses of his memory store the image of his ex rose up. Sweet Magda had not been born to live the life of a sweeper's wife and had left him. When he had been in the throes of miserable loneliness, he had cursed his fate.

Amadeus felt a nudge on his shoulder. It was Anton holding two filled glasses. "Let's drown our sorrows," he said, flicking his head and indicating Benjamin.

As Anton and Amadeus stood together and watched the scene, an anxious-looking Angelika pushed past. Holding a bunch of old newspapers, and mumbling something about 'my genuine Persian rug', she started to spread the pages out on the floor all around Benjamin.

In the silence, which had descended over Angelika's drawing room, they could hear Benjamin beat a hasty retreat. Crumpling up the sheets of paper, as he stepped backwards towards the door, he kept repeating, "So sorry." Each time he said it, he seemed to shrink more. He stopped at the door, gave a hollow laugh, and addressing everyone, he said, "Didn't mean to disrupt the party. Only came to explain. I'm really sorry." Diminished, he smiled awkwardly, and left.

"You know, of course, Benjamin's afraid," said Anton. "He doesn't want anybody to know. That's why he resigned from his post in the orchestra, in case he's going to be investigated."

Anton emptied his glass in one gulp. "Benjamin is afraid of his own shadow. I told him to wait and see. 'It's easy for you to say,' he told me, 'you didn't get involved'."

Amadeus's finger traced the curve of his glass, then looking fixedly at Anton, he said softly, "According to Benjamin, in 1985 I said, and I quote, 'I don't know how these murderers can sleep at night (guards at the Berlin Wall who shoot to kill). It's against human rights but Filthy Ed (von Schnitzler) will stand the truth on his head in his TV programme. This Communist criminal is in good company with Mielke and Honecker'."

Amadeus took a deep breath, then exhaled. "There was more…"

"Yeah…" Anton sighed. He started staring into space. Eventually, taking Amadeus by the elbow, he urged, "Come on, let's have another drink."

# Schulz

# The Dear Boy

Looking up at the small window, which allowed a latticed patch of sunlight to be reflected onto his cell wall, Schulz was day-dreaming. He pictured the world beyond his present confines.

It was the spring of 1995, and as he sat on his hard mattress and leaned back against the whitewashed wall, he saw himself strolling along the Promenadenring of Aschersleben. New, still untainted leaves were rustling in the clear March air. The sparse foliage made it possible to behold the remnants of the medieval fortifications.

It being a Sunday afternoon, plenty of people were out taking their constitutional. He imagined that every so often he raised his hat in greeting, to friends, acquaintances, as well as admiring passers-by. They all seemed to be showering him with goodwill and respect. A couple of children skipping past even stopped briefly by his side, slid their little hands into his and while asking for eyewitness cops and robbers tales proceeded to swing their, and his, arms to and fro like pendulums.

The metallic scrape of the peephole cover on the other side of the door propelled Schulz, none too gently, back to reality. The happy smile on his lips extinguished like a lit match sizzles in contact with cold water.

What would the court decide tomorrow? If found guilty, he could – so his defending counsel had warned – expect up to five years imprisonment. "Five years at my age," he had gasped, "that would finish me." He was seventy and his health was failing.

Schulz was worried, and so he should be. While professing his innocence in court, he knew very well that he had committed the offence of fraud as charged.

Acutely aware that he was being watched he suppressed a resigned smile. He had woken up very early this morning – his monotonous but loud rumblings must have been responsible for that. In his lonely cell he had heard himself say: "I don't feel guilty. If I were, then…" Then what? Still half asleep, he had savoured the implied message and resorted to wishful thinking. Over and over again he had repeated to himself: *if I were guilty I would feel guilty, and I don't feel guilty, therefore I'm not.* Rehearsing this hare-brained mantra had given him moments of solace.

Another scraping sound came from the direction of the peephole cover, and the warden's eye was no longer watching.

Isolated, Schulz was soon brooding again about his fate. How had he got into this fix?

Confined in this cell, for weeks, months on end he had had plenty of time to chew over the situation; like a dog with a bone he could not stop gnawing. Except that he did not get down to the marrow; his facility to dispel thoughts of guilt as soon as they arose prevented it. Being a master in the art of blinding himself to his wrongdoings he had concentrated instead on the sweet game of blaming others and revelled in it.

Had it not been for that devilish cow (as he privately referred to Frau Niklas), in league with that fucking daughter of hers, Anni, he would never have got himself into the shit he was in. These two were at the root of his misfortune. Without that fiasco of his interrogation of the Niklas woman, way back in 1956, he would, firstly, not have fallen foul of his superior. Secondly, Gerda would not have left him. Thirdly, the motive to bribe his son for affection would not have arisen. Therefore, taking all things together, he would not have needed to perpetrate the deed he stood accused of.

"Raus," Schulz had hissed at the end of the interrogation, seething with suppressed anger. His face had been white, blotched with purple, as he hustled Anni and her mother back to the reception of the Aschersleben police station. Without looking around to see whether his two charges were keeping up with him, he tore along the dark and forbidding corridors of the dilapidated building, situated across the courtyard from the reception and reserved for the political cases.

He continued through the same defunct office, which all three of them had crossed five hours earlier on their way to the special interview room. As before they waded amongst the tattered folders strewn everywhere over the floor, as well as the broken glass and crockery. The women walked in single file to pass the remains of a desk, which had been pushed against one wall. Frau Niklas reached up and, in mutinous defiance, knocked against the frayed cord holding a single low-powered light bulb from the ceiling. Schulz did not notice the frantic swaying of the cord and probably would not have cared to register it in his haste to be rid off mother and daughter.

Anni, who had accompanied her mother to the police station, had refused to go home like a good girl and insisted, under threat of creating a scene, on staying with her. Though in the event, Anni was not present during the interrogation. Schulz had locked her into the connecting room.

Taking two steps at a time, the fuming policeman rushed down the flight of stairs and across the yard. The door slammed shut in the women's faces and they had to push it open to enter the corridor to the reception desk, and to freedom.

In his tiny office the hefty policeman collapsed into his chair. "Arrogant, lying bitch and that fucking daughter of hers," he cursed. Thundering out further choice expletives seemed to ease the accumulated sweltering rage of the man.

Nevertheless, other worrisome thoughts entered his head. He knew that he would be called to his superior to report on this afternoon's interrogation. Schulz had been so confident about the outcome that he had gloated to his boss in anticipation of success. It was sod's law that things had not gone his way. "Fucking cows," he cursed again. How on earth would he explain today's blunder to Major Spitz without letting his hoped-for promotion slip through his fingers?

Schulz brewed himself a strong coffee and tried to think up an explanation. He had a date with Gerda later in the evening and knew he would not get the chance to work out his story.

He had already told the major about the interception of a parcel from the West addressed to the local resident, Frau Niklas, which for padding on top of the food items contained a copy of *Der Spiegel*. And to compound the – in the eyes of the East Germans – criminality of the package, each item in it had been wrapped in further unlawful Western newsprint.

Schulz's idea had been to leave the magazine and other newsprint in the parcel and to let it through with the aim of setting a trap. "All I have to do now is sit and wait," he said to the boss, who was dubious about his underling's choice of action.

Shaking his head, Major Spitz had remarked that he didn't believe in handing back evidence. "Confrontation is my motto," he said, "but you didn't ask my advice."

When, after a couple of days, Schulz received an anonymous letter concerning furtive happenings inside the Café Vienna, he was delighted. Apparently, Frau Niklas had been observed handing over some kind of journal to a certain Herr Klein.

The suspicions of the letter writer had been aroused by the secretiveness of the goings-on. The nameless snooper had just happened to pass by in the street. Through a gap in the curtain of the display window – while no other customer was in the shop vicinity – Frau Niklas had allegedly first carefully looked all around and then kept watch while Herr Klein hastily hid 'what looked like a journal or magazine' in his briefcase.

Schulz had felt vindicated and, unable to keep the latest development to himself, had boasted to the major, "That stupid bitch will squeal. Sorry, Frau Niklas will talk, you'll see." Grinning conspiratorially, and rubbing his hands, he had breathed, "I have my ways and means."

But Frau Niklas turned out to be tougher than anticipated. Schulz eventually resorted to intimidation. But she stood her ground, insisting that she had never handed anything to Herr Klein.

Schulz called her 'a bloody liar' and threatened to put Anni into care. "I can make you talk," he said menacingly and told her, 'to think about it'. Then he laughed and said that he had 'all the time in the world'.

In spite of the strong-arm tactics, the only thing Frau Niklas eventually admitted to was that, yes – claiming that she had only just remembered it – she had given something to Herr Klein: a copy of his *Church News* which he regularly edited and produced. And, oh yes, there had been a copy of *Der Spiegel* in a recent parcel. But that magazine she professed to have burnt. "Of course, I burnt it," she said, and she had banged her fist on the table and shouted, "If that's a crime, what the hell is this country coming to?!"

Schulz was furious, but he had no evidence to disprove her. A co-ordinated search at Herr Klein's had not come up with any illegal material.

As Schulz finished drinking his strong coffee, sitting slouched in his office chair, intermittently still swearing aloud at that Niklas woman, he grew increasingly apprehensive about the forthcoming confrontation with Major Spitz.

Whichever way Schulz presented the case, he would appear incompetent or stupid, or both. *I have been had*, he repeated to himself. *Why didn't I pull her in and confront her with the bloody magazine…?*

"You're quiet this evening," Gerda observed between mouthfuls of the special meal she had prepared and beautifully set out on her best damask tablecloth.

"Whatever is the matter with you, Kasparchen?" She was all excited about her piece of news for Schulz, but seeing that he was distracted she thought that she would wait with it.

"Trouble at the office?" she inquired as she brought in the sweet dish.

"No, everything's all right." He wanted to forget his problem for a bit and had no intention to discuss it. In any case, his work was taboo. So he made some effort and brightened up, before falling back into gloom.

"I think I'd better go, I'm not good company." He pointed to the stain where he had just spilled some of his coffee. "So sorry."

Gerda was still bursting to tell him her news, but she was not going to say anything. Not while he was sitting there with The-I-Couldn't-Care-About-You-Demeanour on display. Thwarted in her objective, she had become angry. "You have no etiquette," she said. "The dinner took me hours, yet you didn't notice what you were eating. Don't know why I bothered, I'm sure." Her cheeks were flushed and she shot him a blazing look from her dark eyes. "Go on, go home then. You might as well not be here."

"I changed my mind." Suddenly Schulz was all smiles. Desire had made him forget the Niklas-problem. He stood behind her as she piled up the plates and dishes on the table. Embracing her, he started kissing the back of her neck. Tomorrow was years away.

She tried to free herself. "Let go, I say! That's all I am good for, is it?" When he kept drawing her closer, she told him, "Look, I am not in the mood."

"Come on, love. Don't play hard to get." By now Schulz was on fire. In the past she had never refused him and her rebuff now excited him all the more. He picked her up, and ignoring her pleas, as well as hefty kicks to his legs, carried her to the living-room sofa, which at night served as her bed.

The more she objected, the more pleasure it gave him to subdue her. All the while he experienced an uncanny feeling of relief, comparable, as he thought, to shackles bursting open. When she bit his hand, which he had pushed over her mouth to stop her screams, he slapped her with brutal force. Part of him registered horror at what he was doing, but it was not enough to stop him.

Schulz was never to see Gerda again. When he came back a week later to apologize, she was gone. Peering through the now curtain-less windows of the flat, he could see it was empty of all furniture.

Where had she gone? She had not contacted him. There was no message for him at the police station. Her neighbours professed not to know her whereabouts.

"I am no longer her guardian, I'm afraid I can't help," was what her mother said, frostily. Noticing the open hostility in her eyes, Schulz did not press her for an answer, even though he thought she knew where Gerda was.

Because he felt ashamed and rather wanted to forget about the whole sordid thing, he did not get his colleagues involved in a search for Gerda. And he, for his part, did not try very hard to find her. It was easier not to have to face her. Anyway, he told himself, she had not shown much give, considering how many times she had declared her love for him.

After a while, he convinced himself it was her hard luck that she did not want to know him. He had been ready to apologize… . Circumstances had driven him to lose his cool. Bloody Niklas bitch!

※

Fifteen years later Schulz was contacted out of the blue. A young man or boy had apparently telephoned and asked for him by name at the station. He had left a contact number. His name was Benedikt.

"Saint Benedikt, eh, I see," sneered Schulz as he took the scrap of paper with the details from his boss's hand.

Major Spitz was no longer in charge. He had retired five years ago. Good riddance, Schulz had thought; any new broom had to be an improvement.

Under the new man, Klaus — everybody called him by the first name — Schulz had prospered. Major Spitz never forgave him the fiasco with Frau Niklas, but Klaus appreciated Schulz's zeal and independent decisions.

Klaus was happy to let Schulz get on with things as long as he, Klaus, had time to pursue his activities, chasing skirts being the favourite amongst those. He had rewarded Schulz by giving him a leg-up on the job ladder. Schulz's ability to write concise reports had come in for particular praise. And, proving the old adage, 'success breeds success', his manifold qualities had come to the attention of the Stasi hierarchy, and they had approached Schulz for his co-operation.

Anyway, the years under Klaus were, as Schulz was later to call them, 'my golden years'. True, on the personal front, things could have been more complete — he lacked a wife and family — but, as he was fond of saying: "Being a bachelor has its compensations." If Schulz's coarse laugh, which usually followed this pronouncement, was considered repulsive by some, they did not say so.

❦

"I am Benedikt," said the youngster who had entered the office and stood by the door. "I couldn't talk over the telephone…"

Schulz invited Benedikt to sit down in the visitor's chair. There was something familiar about the lad. Where had he seen those eyes before?

"All right, you tell it to me straight. We are private here. I must say, I'm very interested." Schulz smiled as he leaned back, making the chair creak under his weight. He had put on the jolly tone of voice, as for some reason he felt kindly disposed to the kid. These eyes, they reminded him… bugger, if he knew of whom.

"My mother, Gerda Ehrlich, told me to come to you. She said that you would know…once you saw me…" Benedikt kept hesitating, seemingly uncertain. "She told me in hospital, before she died… . She had been in a car accident. That was seven months ago now. She made me promise…you would know, she said." Benedikt looked up and across: "She said that you are my father and I have a right to know."

Schulz's thoughts and feelings were in turmoil. Gerda, of course! The boy had her eyes. But dead! She had been so full of life. So young, and dead! He kept shaking his head in disbelief. Then it struck home: *Gerda sent the boy to me. Her son! Our son! Fucking hell, I've got a son!*

Schulz got up so fast that the chair toppled over. The next moment he crouched down beside Benedikt and hugged him. "Your mother wants me to take care of you." Tears were welling up in Schulz's eyes. "You did right to come to me. Don't you worry, you are safe with me, son." Wiping his wet cheeks, but laughing, he stretched to full height. "My son," he murmured. "A son of my own."

Opening his office door, he shouted, "Stop all calls!" To the girl at the reception, he said, "I'm busy right now, top priority."

Coming back into the office, he pulled the overturned chair up from the floor and took up position behind his desk again. He wanted to know all about Benedikt and Gerda. Where had they lived, how had Gerda supported herself and her son? – Benedikt confirmed that there had only ever been the two of them.

It pleased Schulz that she had never married. It meant no divided loyalty for the lad.

Where had Benedikt gone to school, Schulz asked, and what were the boy's plans for the future? Who had been looking after him since his mother's death?

The questions kept on coming, and the longer Schulz spent with Benedikt the more he liked the young lad in front of him. He appeared to be intelligent, he was well-spoken, responsive without being sentimental, grown up for his years. Gerda had done a good job and, apparently, she had not sown grudges.

Benedikt, so both agreed, would remain at the Sport Academy where he was a boarder, but he would travel from Rostock to Aschersleben whenever he was free.

"There's only one problem with my visits," the youngster ventured; he seemed embarrassed and blushed. "I'll need something towards my train fares." Having been more than reassured about the necessary cash, he later quipped, much more confidently, "And maybe a little extra on top for expenses. And, oh yes, Dad, I could do with a new pair of trainers."

True, at first, Schulz had been a little taken aback by the request for money – after all he had no experience of subsidizing offspring – but then he thought it only right and proper. He was not going to skimp on a son of his. He would do him proud. And as he gloried in Benedikt's adoring glances, he kept recalling Gerda's devastating eyes. If only he had found her!

Clearly, Benedikt was showing enterprise, something that in Schulz's opinion was worthy of reward. 'The apple does not fall far from the tree'; Schulz reminded himself of this saying as he looked proprietarily at the dear boy.

But before long Benedikt's wish list grew alarmingly. Schulz knew that he was being over-indulgent, it was just that he hated to see the light go out in the boy's eyes.

In the autumn of 1972, about a year after the youngster had entered Schulz's life, he found himself hard-pressed to satisfy the boy's latest requirement. Within months of purchasing the racy five-gear bicycle, he had been asked for a second-hand moped. Of that too Benedikt was now tiring and he was eyeing-up a newish Trabant car a friend's father planned to sell.

"As soon as I pass the driving test I'll need to be mobile; until then we can garage the car," Benedikt had declared. "Think how everybody will envy me a father like you. You're the best."

When Schulz doubted whether he could afford the money, the boy just laughed. "Dad, you practically run the police station, you must earn a good salary. And," he winked conspiratorially, "there's your bonus from the Stasi. It's due next week, am I right?"

Schulz knew that he should not have let on about his connection. He had not mentioned it to anybody before, but the boy had got under his skin. When he looked at the boy's dark eyes, Schulz felt the need for veneration. The thought of incurring his son's disregard had the power to make him feel physically sick.

Around the time the Trabant issue came up, the opportunity to earn 'a little extra on the side' had presented itself. Very timely, as Schulz thought. Some Stasi chums from further afield had cottoned on to the idea of copying the Ministry of State Security practice of demanding ransom money from West Germany in exchange for political prisoners.

Of course Schulz and the others only pretended to buy the freedom of the prisoners. They were in no position to buy anybody. But they had no scruples.

As far as Schulz was concerned, he deceived Frau Lichtblick – amongst others – into believing that the name of her son would be put on a special list of prisoners awaiting selection for freedom. However, once she had paid the bribe over she heard nothing more and her son served his sentence.

Had the East German State not crumbled, Schulz would have got away with his scheme. But the Berlin Wall fell and Frau Lichtblick's inquiries established that he was the person who had swindled her out of money and property. That was despite the fact that he had not used his own name in his dealings with her.

As soon as Schulz entered the Berlin courtroom to hear finally what the future held for him, he looked out for Benedikt. But why was somebody else occupying his usual seat? Where was his son?

Today of all days Schulz had counted on him to be there. Disappointment gave way to annoyance. He had unfailingly attended the previous sessions. Where the hell was he? After everything he had done for the boy. If traffic had delayed him… . He should have allowed extra time. If the shoe had been on the other foot, he, Schulz, would have made sure he was here.

Half an hour passed and still there was no sign of Benedikt. Why had he absented himself from his father's life? Had he deserted him?

In forlorn hope, Schulz scanned the faces of the few latecomers. Again and again he scrutinised the sea of people. Several women in a small group raised their fists in anger when they noticed him staring at them. Anyway, he just gazed unblinkingly back at them.

He thought one of the red-faced women was Frau Lichtblick who, as he knew, had started the proceedings against him. Well, she had been worth a few bob. Why shouldn't he have taken advantage? He began mumbling, "You stupid b…." but stopped short of completing the well-oiled phrase. Somehow he could not be bothered…

The various barristers went through their paces but Schulz could not concentrate. He kept missing chunks of what they were saying and hence lost track of the arguments. He pinched himself to wake up from what seemed a horrid twilight state, but soon his attention drifted away again. What if Benedikt was not here through no fault of his own? Something dreadful could have happened to him. What if he was ill, unable to travel. He could be lying injured somewhere at the side of a road.

By the time Schulz and his co-defendants were being returned to prison to start their respective sentences – he had been given thirty months – he was worried out of his mind. He who normally lacked imagination conjured up pictures and story lines a fiction writer could have appreciated.

Three weeks on, Schulz still had no news from his son. His nights in particular were filled with frantic worry. He had difficulties sleeping and, as had become the norm, he was tossing and turning on his mattress.

A thought struck him like lightening: *Frau Lichtblick must have suffered the way he was now when she didn't know where her son had disappeared to after we arrested him*. Astonished, he sat up with a jerk; sympathy with a victim had never before entered his head. "Shit," he groaned, it was three months before we let her know…

Bathed in sweat a resolution ripened. He would write to her and apologise. His barrister would pass on the letter.

After a while Schulz felt calmer, and, at the point of dozing off, the, to him, at any other time, ridiculous conviction took hold that his goodwill would curry favours with the gods and he would hear from his son.

The next afternoon, Schulz was stuffing his letter to Frau Lichtblick into an envelope, when the warden entered. "You've a visitor. Come along."

Schulz did not move. "Who…?" he stammered.

"On yer feet, prisoner 583. Haven't all day. You'll find out."

Thank God, was Schulz's first thought. "At last," he mumbled indistinctly. Even before the door to the visiting room was pushed fully open, he had caught a glimpse of Benedikt. Having rushed past the warden, smiling at Schulz from behind a long bare wooden table was the sun-tanned face of the dear boy. Next to him there were at least half a dozen more chairs, all empty.

The officer on duty pointed to the chair opposite Benedikt and as Schulz sat down he felt an unburdening as if a heavy cargo was being dumped. Behind him he heard the warden click the door shut.

"How are you, Dad?"

Schulz was all smiles. He pushed his hands halfway across the table, offering them. But Benedikt kept his elbows stiffly on the sides of his chair.

"Why didn't you turn up?" said Schulz, looking fully at his son.

He seemed taken aback by his father's direct question and looked down.

Disillusioned, Schulz started very slowly to lean back, making a scratching sound as he withdrew his hands from the table.

Benedikt blushed. Seemingly uncomfortable he blinked several times. Then, avoiding his father's gaze, he said, "I'm sorry I wasn't there to hear the sentencing. I rang up and found out from your barrister. You see, I, I mean we, we were away in Greece, on holiday."

"On holiday," Schulz echoed. He shook himself like a rain-drenched dog. With his mouth falling open he looked and sounded like a mental retard.

"Let me explain. Look. You and I knew what the outcome would be, didn't we? Well, more or less at least. I couldn't have done anything to change it, could I? You only got thirty months and—"

"Only thirty," Schulz interrupted, confused and shaking his head.

"Well, yes," continued Benedikt, quickly, as not to give his father a chance to say more. "And your barrister thinks you'll be out before then. Anyway, Regina had booked this holiday some time ago. We didn't think that it would clash with the case."

While Benedikt drew breath, Schulz gasped, "Regina?"

"I must've told you about her, my new girlfriend, partner actually, from Hamburg. We also work in the same school." Having taken Schulz's inquiry as a signal to move away from the topic of his court absence, Benedikt visibly relaxed.

He knew very well that he had not mentioned Regina, mainly because of her rather right-wing political views. "Anyway," he continued, "I'm sure you'll like her, once you get to know her. She's very attached to me."

Benedikt's sudden appearance, the unforeseen news – it was all a bit much for Schulz. Shut away in his cell, his thinking processes had slowed down. He knew he would need to dissect everything at his leisure. There was one thing though he, right now, keenly felt. Despite Benedikt not having filled him in about his holiday plans, he was not bitter. It surprised him. Three weeks ago he would not have been so accommodating. Sparks would have been flying, Schulz told himself. All that mattered to him now was that his son was here. How handsome he looked…

"Regina really cares, you know." Benedikt was speaking again. "That's the only reason she wants me to cut down on my visits to you. She thinks, if the media got to know about it, it would harm my promotion." Benedikt flashed a most dazzling smile. "You see, I have applied for the headship. You taught me to be ambitious." When there was no response from Schulz, Benedikt lowered his voice to a whisper: "Actually, she doesn't know that I am here with you."

For long minutes Schulz did not say anything. What could he say? Benedikt's words hurt. That he could not deny. Not wanting to show his pain, he turned away.

"Dad, I'm sorry, I…"

"No," Schulz gestured for Benedikt to stop, "I am sorry that I've become a liability to you. In your place…why wouldn't you break all contact? That would serve me right!" He shook his head and gave a resigned sigh. "Just remember one thing. Follow your heart. That's what I should've done. You see, there was another me before I joined the police and became a Stasi. Your mother sensed it. Then I had to destroy it all."

Father and son sat facing each other. As if on command they reached out for one another.

*Bloc III*

## Bertrand

# A Most Magnificent Peacock

It was the afternoon of the Preview; in a few hours time Bertrand's London exhibition was going to open and the invited guests would crowd around his thirty most recent paintings.

Bertrand who had only this morning arrived from Hong Kong for the occasion was now – after a short rest in his hotel – inspecting one of the two interconnected rooms of the prestigious Holland Park Gallery. He walked along the rows of pictures like a general inspecting his troops, but he stopped here and there and winced as he noticed flaws jumping out at him. Why had he not detected those back home in his studio before the paintings had been shipped out? If only he could still make changes!

"Don't even think about it." The jolly voice of his agent, Georgio, made Bertrand jump and spin around.

Georgio, who had tiptoed into the room and observed

Bertrand mutter and shake his head while sweeping his arm sideways as if wanting to overpaint something on the large oil before him, had drawn the obvious conclusion.

The next moment Georgio was hugging Bertrand affectionately, "It's good to see you in the flesh. Must be ages since you came here last. But –" he downcast his eyes " – I didn't mean to interrupt your precious moments of contemplation, except Martha from reception gave me a note for you."

"A letter?" Sounding surprised, Bertrand accepted the white envelope and turned it over. There was no sender's name on the back.

"Well," said Georgio, "Martha thought that the well-spoken man in blue overalls who came in this morning with the letter was a fellow countryman of yours, at least if not Malaysian then Indian. He also looked rather self-conscious, she thought."

Bertrand was none the wiser. "Not many uninitiated know that I'm in London," he remarked as he pocketed the mysterious letter.

※

An hour later, Bertrand was back in his hotel room. While undressing to take a shower before getting himself ready for the opening night, the letter Georgio had handed him earlier at the Gallery fell out of his shirt pocket.

As soon as he picked it up, Bertrand felt somehow uneasy. He prided himself on being rational and dismissed premonitions as so much mumbo-jumbo. Why then did the envelope seem to be burning his fingers?

Somebody of Asian appearance had handed it in, could it have been…? No, surely not? Too long ago! Bertrand dismissed the possibility. He should have asked Martha about the man's age and for a description. It would have given him a clue and no doubt put his mind at rest.

If only the nightmares had not started again. Now, why should that be? Having stepped out of the circle, which his discarded pieces of clothing had formed on the carpet, Bertrand passed the envelope from thumb and index finger of one hand to the other as if it were a strange object and he did not know what to do with it. Then, having made up his mind, with a stern expression on his face, he slotted one finger under the flap and almost brutally split it open.

He blanched. There it was, at the top of the single typewritten page, the form of address: *Dear Bertie.*

Bertrand's heart missed a beat. Alistair? Who else! Not many people had called him Bertie. His parents had, but they were no longer alive. Two cousins, but he had lost touch with them. An awful long time in the past there had been one other...

Once Bertrand had controlled the tremor of his hand, he read on. *I hope* – apologised the letter writer – *that you don't mind the familiar address. It is what I called you fifty years ago. I want you to think back to 3rd September 1942!*

With a shriek Bertrand let himself sink into the deep oversized hotel armchair.

As he had feared...

The sheet of paper, read and re-read, floated to the floor.

All colour drained from Bertrand's face. He had tried so hard for so long to erase that day from his memory. Soon after the incident, before Bertrand left his parents' rubber plantation to attend boarding school, he and Ali – as Bertrand had called his friend then – had vowed never ever to refer to that day. They had also agreed not to meet again and not to seek each other out. Should they happen to come across one another by chance, they were to act like strangers.

Bertrand kept shaking his head. Why was his one-time bosom friend who had lived on the neighbouring estate contacting him now? How was it, he puzzled, that recent dreams which had foretold a meeting were about to come true…?

Bertrand levered himself out of the hotel chair. He started pacing the room. Unclothed, his slight figure looked bereft, like a shorn sheep robbed of its fleece.

Maybe it had been by chance that Ali had found him. He could have come to London and read about the exhibition or even passed the gallery and seen the name of his childhood friend advertised. He may have decided half a century was long enough to honour their teenage vow.

*I imagine*, Ali had written, seemingly tongue in cheek, *you are 'hit' with recognition (?!) and furious with me? Am I right, or am I right?* Despite being in turmoil, Bertrand had to smile: still the joker he used to know, it seemed.

The image of the fourteen-year old Alistair, Ali, flashed through his mind. His friend had been the taller one, heavier boned, his skin lighter. But then, Ali had some Scottish blood running in his veins. His maternal grandfather had been born on Orkney but was, as a young man, sent to Kuala Lumpur as an administrator. On one of his trips into the rainforest he had met and fallen for the beautiful daughter of a Malay landowner. They married and eventually he got to manage the generation-old rubber plantation. Granddad Hamish had died of a fever before Ali was born. His devoted grandmother had kept her late husband's kilt, sporran and bagpipes, as well as photographs and pictures of his Scottish homeland. She always wore a miniature portrait of her Hamish in a locket around her neck.

Even now Bertrand remembered how envious he had

always been of Ali's roots. How could his family tree compete with a grandfather who had worn a kilt and played bagpipes? All of his forefathers had been boring Malay landowners. His parents' larger estate did not compensate for Ali's exotic family history.

From earliest childhood the two boys had been inseparable. Ever since they had been able to walk they had played together, until that dark day in September when Bertrand had killed, and Ali had been there when it happened. Nothing on earth would ever bring the old villager back to life.

Annoyance rose in Bertrand. Why should Ali need or want to remind him? And if he felt he had to, why do it in such a brutally direct way?

After old Mr Chan, who worked as a handyman for Bertrand's parents, had gone missing, there had been a search. It had not taken long to find his dead body. An investigation had followed. The police had interviewed the local villagers, as well as the workers on the estates – and the boys' parents. But nobody had questioned the youngsters. They were still thought of as children.

The general consensus was that Chan had been killed by either Japanese soldiers of the occupational forces out on reconnaissance or by isolated Communist terrorists who might have been disturbed in a hiding place at the edge of the rainforest.

Bertrand, who had sat down again in the hotel armchair, picked the sheet of paper up from the floor and once more scrutinized it. But apart from the handwritten signature and a PS stating Ali's intention to attend the Preview later this evening, there was nothing Bertrand had not noted earlier. No address, no telephone number.

It briefly occurred to Bertrand that he could leave word

with the Gallery reception not to admit Ali. But what was the point? It would only delay their meeting. The Gallery staff could not forbid Ali to wait outside in the street. Now that he had taken the trouble to write he was not going to disappear.

The ringing of the telephone made Bertrand jump. No, it was not Ali, just Georgio wanting to confirm the title of the oil painting Bertrand had earlier on taken issue with.

Anyway, a glance at his watch stirred Bertrand into action. He took the delayed shower, dressed and ordered a taxi to Holland Park.

※

During the slow journey in heavy traffic, Bertrand seemed to have forgotten the Preview altogether.

Weariness had spread to his mind and body. He leaned against the headrest and as he shut his eyes he saw himself on that fateful day carrying the revolver he had taken from his father's safe, which was hidden in the wall behind one of his bookcases. The Japanese soldiers had not found the weapon when they had searched the estate soon after occupying the neighbourhood.

The revolver had felt unyielding in his trouser pocket, hurting the inside of his thigh as it knocked against it. He knew he must not be seen carrying the weapon. But being in possession of it was bound to make their mission, code-named RESCUE, much more authentic.

As he had many times before, Bertrand visualised the sequence of events on that afternoon of the 3rd September. "Maybe it's already too late," Suresh, the Indian cook had muttered while Bertrand was stuffing handfuls of grains and seeds into a paper bag. The Buddha-like cook, hands folded across his middle, had shifted his head from side to side as he disclosed, "Chan go to forest to stop noise. 'Fed up,' he said, 'the noise be their death'."

Suresh's tip-off had panicked Bertrand. "We've got to get there first," he told Ali, "quick," and started to run. Rushing furiously ahead, he kept turning his head to check that Ali was following. "We've got to scare them away," Bertrand panted and to himself he mumbled, "Good job I've got the shooter."

Bertrand was aware that Mr Chan detested the loud and unpleasant voices of the birds, which avowedly, were particularly annoying in the late afternoons while they were going to roost, calling out as they moved from lower to higher tree branches.

*If only I had appreciated the full fury of Chan's hatred,* Bertrand thought, stifling a groan. *Wise after the event...maybe if he...*

"Are you all right, gov?" The driver's voice penetrated Bertrand's speculations. "Only you look in pain."

"No, I'm fine," Bertrand reassured the man. "Thanks." But before long he was lost again in his thoughts.

As Bertrand recalled, by the time he and Ali – by now the boys had slowed down to stalking pace – heard Chan's characteristic wheezing coming from some bushes in front, he indicated that they stop. As he and Ali did so, a sight of exceptional beauty made Bertrand forget all about the rescue mission. With his arms hanging limp by his side, he just stood, motionless, overcome...

Only steps away, on a clearing in the forest a most magnificent peacock was displaying his brilliant ornamental feathers. The upper tail feathers formed a long train that covered any plain feathers underneath. That particular peacock, flown in from somewhere, it seemed, had assumed leadership and was performing to a female by raising the train and spreading it like a fan. Other peahens were scratching in the soil in anticipation of food.

As the boys both watched – Ali was similarly affected by the sight – they both stood perfectly still. Then, in front of them, a twig snapped. The birds too had heard it and were alerted. The male lifted its bronze-coloured plumage on the head, neck and body.

Through a curtain of leaves, Bertrand saw that Mr Chan was raising a rifle.

Old and rusty though it looked, the boy did not doubt its destructive power. He was horrified.

"No!" he screamed. There could be nothing more beautiful and majestic and the image of the peacock, lifeless and blood-splattered on the ground, was unbearable to him. Instantly he lifted his revolver, intending to shoot in the air and to scare the flock of birds away.

He could not have predicted it, but the handyman who had been crouching in the bushes, stood up to full height the very moment Bertrand fired. The bullet hit him at the back of his head.

It had all happened so fast. When Chan keeled over Bertrand was aghast. Kneeling next to the dead body, he was inconsolable.

"What have you done?" murmured Ali once the birds had all flown off in their lumbering manner.

"How exciting to meet a childhood friend after half a century," Anni blurted out, after Bertrand had explained about the curiously dressed man of retirement age who had walked up to him and her. But almost immediately, she wished she had kept quiet.

Why the forced smiles? The tension seemed palpable and Anni was puzzled. Alistair did not fit the picture of 'my long lost friend' as per Bertrand's introduction. Something was not right, instead of hugging each other from pleasure about their reunion the two men eyed each other as gladiators might have done before a fight. Flanking each other, they both seemed to be measuring an adversary.

Other Preview guests risked surreptitious glances at the latecomer. His ill-fitting black suit strained against shoulders and hips. The shirtsleeves protruded from the cuffs.

A borrowed suit or one Alistair had outgrown, Anni thought. It would have been better if he'd turned up in working clothes. Alas, his choice of words and upper-class manner suggested to her that he would have felt the need to dress appropriately.

"Wait for me," Bertrand managed to say before Georgio took his arm to guide him away from Ali towards a group of fans.

Eventually the Preview Night was coming to an end. Anni and Alistair went outside and continued talking near the still brightly lit gallery windows. Their conversation circled around Bertrand's show.

The exhibition pieces were a representative sample of his usual range, mythical oriental beasts and felines, as well as emaciated figures with hollowed faces. They both favoured the same painting of a Siamese cat.

Ali wondered how she had made Bertrand's acquaintance and she recounted how she had met the artist at her friends' party in Düsseldorf and how interested Bertrand had been in her Stasi-dominated past and the fall of the Berlin Wall. But as soon as she referred to his and Ali's childhood friendship, the shutters came down over Ali's face.

When Bertrand finally appeared, Anni thanked him for the invitation to the opening night, and after some small talk she excused herself.

Left to themselves the two friends felt less self-conscious and exchanged a long overdue handshake.

"Look," Ali said, "do me a favour…for old time's sake?"

While Bertrand scraped his shoe over the pavement, he tried not to think of ulterior motives on Ali's part. "Yes…if I can," he replied hesitantly.

"Come to my digs for a coffee. Will you?" But Ali did not allow Bertrand time for a potential refusal and carried on speaking, "If we go now there's plenty of time for you to catch the tube back to your hotel. I know where you're staying. Anni told me," he added, probably because he had noticed a look of alarm in Bertrand's eyes.

Despite misgivings, Bertrand agreed to Ali's invitation. A meeting in a public place, the next day, would have been safer, he thought and right away felt ashamed. What a coward he was! *This is my old friend*, he reprimanded himself. *He's not likely to beat me up, is he?*

Nevertheless, other suspicions surfaced: what of the possibility of blackmail? There was Ali's shabby appearance… . If he were to talk…the papers love to cut down anyone with a bit of a name.

As Bertrand gave his friend a calculating stare, he responded with a sunny smile of old and Bertrand felt reassured. In the spur of the moment he gave Ali a hug.

"I want you to see something," he heard Ali say.

"Yes, all right," said Bertrand. "By the way, there's no need to worry about the tube. I'll get Tony to drive us." Bertrand took a few steps to a waiting car at the curbside and leant into the lowered window.

"You'll have to direct Tony to your place," said Bertrand once the two friends had settled in the back of the car.

During the twenty minutes' drive a hush came over everyone. Only now and then was the silence disturbed by Ali's clipped directions.

Having stopped at the entrance to a cul-de-sac, outside what looked like a warehouse of sorts, the friends got out of the car. After Bertrand requested Tony to wait for him, he followed Ali to a padlocked high gate. A Doberman dog appeared at once, but on a word from Ali returned to his kennel in the grounds.

Ali's digs turned out to be a tiny office room with a tea-making facility and a sink. Two doors led off, one – it happened to be ajar – belonged to a toilet and the second one Ali opened and walked through, beckoning Bertrand to follow.

Bertrand entered a bare-looking conservatory with concrete flooring. The glaring light from a fluorescent tube overhead illuminated the dowdy surroundings. There was no furniture, only a tall grey-coloured screen which, as he soon discovered when Ali slid it sideways, hid a sleeping bag on top of an air mattress and a D-I-Y wooden easel. A virgin 24"x16" canvass was perched on a rough improvised holding device. Other canvasses were turned against one of the glazed walls.

Bertrand's interest was immediately aroused. "Aha, that's what you want me to see!" Excitedly, his tiny figure circled around the canvasses. "Your work?"

Ali's bashful nod was greeted with effuse exclamations of delight. Bertrand now felt at home. "A fellow artist. Why didn't you say!" He kept shaking his head in amazement and waved his arms about in an ecstatic manner at the prospect of viewing.

In contrast to his friend, Ali remained subdued. "Just wait one moment," he said and briefly left the conservatory. He returned wheeling the single office stool into the room. "Let the show begin." Even though he had changed over to his and Bertrand's mother tongue, he sounded perfunctory.

As soon as Ali turned the first canvas around, Bertrand was beside himself with joy. Having jumped off the stool, he pranced agitatedly from one corner of the conservatory to the other, before stopping in front of the picture. Scrutinising it from all angles, his face took on an earnest expression. "Brilliant work," he said very quietly.

He continued looking at the oil. It was of a peacock and his three hens. The background suggested the birds' rainforest habitat. "It's the place back home where I…where Chan died, isn't it?"

Ali looked away, but nodded. "I hope it doesn't upset you, the peacock scene, I mean."

He must know it does, Bertrand thought and squeezed his mouth tight. Is that why he referred to the 3rd September in his letter…so that the picture wouldn't come as a complete shock…?

"You never paint birds, I know. I've been following your road to fame. See those," Ali picked up several folders from the floor, "my scrapbooks of most of your exhibitions. I'm your number one fan."

Bertrand felt embarrassed and waved his hand in belittlement of his accomplishments. "Come now, show me your other work."

Ali did not seem in a hurry. Slowly, he took off the black restraining jacket, which was hampering his movements and threw it into one corner. "Didn't think I would have been admitted to your exhibition without it," he snickered. "As it was, it was difficult, with no official invitation card." He focussed on his friend, and an amiable smile replaced the smirk. "But the girl from reception remembered me and let me in. Even though I looked ridiculous." He pointed to the jacket, "It's not even mine. I borrowed it."

An hour later Bertrand had seen all of the work stacked up against the conservatory wall. Looking at the dates next to the initials, A L, it had all been produced during the last eighteen months.

"First I went to Scotland," Alistair said, "to attend a nephew's wedding." Scotland had captivated him and he had stayed on, until the money ran out.

"What about money from back home?" Bertrand asked.

"The plantation ran into debt. My incompetence, I'm afraid," Ali admitted, and because he needed to earn his living he had come to London. "Started work here as a night watchman, ten months ago," he explained, "I'm not meant to live here but the boss chooses to ignore it."

"Such brilliant work, Ali. Puts mine to shame. Didn't you try some galleries?"

"No luck there."

Bertrand was shocked and offered his help. "Don't take it as patronising, but with my name... . I'll get Georgio onto it. What a sorry state of affairs the art world is in..."

Everything was going so well for Ali. Dates were agreed, arrangements discussed. Afterwards the two friends toasted each other's success, clinking their chipped water glasses filled with red plonk.

Then before leaving, Bertrand picked up one of the folders from the floor. He had done it unthinkingly really, and without Ali trying to snatch it away, Bertrand would probably have just put it down again. But Ali's unseemly haste drew Bertrand's attention. "What is it?" he asked and held on. In the ensuing tug of war several watercolours dislodged and slipped out.

As Ali grew pale, the truth dawned on Bertrand. What he was looking at on the concrete flooring reeked of amateur work. He bent down and picked up two crudely executed seascapes, signed with the same initials A L and dated within the last eighteen months, in exactly the same manner as the masterly oils from earlier.

"Why did you pass someone else's work off as your own?" asked Bertrand, his voice hardly audible. His tiny frame seemed to shrink. "Whose are the oils?"

It was some time before Ali answered and Bertrand learned that the paintings were the work of an old boy who occasionally dropped into the art class Ali had been attending since coming to London. Being Scottish, and having lived in the Far East for many years, Alex Louchlin shared interests with Ali and they became friendly. About a month ago, on one of his visits, Ali had found the front door on latch. Entering the hall he had seen Alex lying on the floor. He was dead.

Alistair knew that the old man had no living relatives and while waiting for the doctor to arrive, he had been admiring Alex's artwork. "Some ignoramus would only have thrown the paintings – they were unframed – onto a skip, together with the out-of-date furniture. So I took them," Ali said. "I appreciated them."

Apparently, Alex had based his work on drawings he had made while travelling through India. The peacock scene had originated there.

According to Alistair, Alex Louchlin would have wanted

him to have 'my feathered friends' as he called them. He was well-known as an eccentric, despised money and was not interested in fame.

"When I realised you were exhibiting in Holland Park. Well, certain ideas came into my head. You see, Alex signed his work with the initials A L. My initials, as you know."

"What are we to do?" Bertrand said, sitting once more on the office stool. With his arms crossed over his chest, he was rocking forward and back, again and again. "You can't plagiarize the man's work. It wouldn't be right."

Alistair slowly walked nearer. "I can't, can I!" He stopped within touching distance of Bertrand. Lifting his head to the ceiling, Ali emitted a raucous, piercing sort of a laugh.

Bertrand had never heard anything like it. But it seemed to him that years of accumulated frustration exploded in that single horrid blare, and he intuitively knew that his sheltered existence only afforded an inkling of Alistair's desperation.

"I can't, can I?" Alistair repeated, but now the words formed a question. "You…" he continued, "you who never confessed to killing old Mr Chan, you are lecturing me on what is right." He gave a resigned shrug of his shoulders. "I hoped I wouldn't have to remind you, face to face, that's why I put the date in my letter. Thought it would be enough…"

Alistair's measured delivery chilled Bertrand more than any ranting and raving would have. He looked on in horror as the friend he thought he knew walked back to the stack of paintings, hauled one out and, having flicked a pocket knife open, held it against the canvas.

"I'll deface this and all the others, unless… . It's not the money I need," and looking Bertrand straight in the eyes, Ali said, "I want to be somebody, if only for a little while."

"Please! Don't do anything rash!" Bertrand pleaded – he was convinced Ali's threat was for real. "These paintings are greater than both of us, greater even than old Alex Louchlin."

"Please, Ali," Bertrand whispered, as he walked with outstretched arms closer to his childhood friend. "Remember, my and your guilt will die with us but these paintings must live. Whatever the criminality! D'you understand what I'm saying?

"Against our wrongdoing the paintings tip the scales, any day."

Alistair let go of the knife.

# *Helga*

## *Impressions*

Helga brushed some cake crumbs off the front of her crisp, white cotton blouse and pushed her empty coffee cup and plate to the far edge of the marble-effect table. Next to her, engrossed in his favourite computer magazine, husband Wulf was oblivious to her presence.

From below the table's screwed-down column, she got hold of her bulging handbag, slung it across her knees and began fishing for the tattered old diary she had only recently rescued. Together with other bits and pieces it had fallen out of an old biscuit tin, labelled 'English Mementos'. Rubber bands held the diary's binding together; once she had removed those, a stack of yellowing pages spilled onto the table.

She picked up the top one and read the heading: *NOVEMBER 1961, ON BOARD THE OSTENDE-DOVER FERRY.*

Helga had not opened the long-forgotten diary since her stay in England, forty-two years ago and was looking forward to read about her erstwhile thoughts and observations. It somehow seemed fitting that she should delve into the old entries while on her second channel crossing, again in November.

Thinking back to her first trip, she hardly noticed the clink of cups and plates as they were being cleared from her and Wulf's table; in any case, the deep carpet had masked the waiter's approach. The suave surroundings on today's ferryboat encouraged comparisons with the basic outfit back then. Green deckchairs and wooden benches were definitely out.

Just as on her first visit to England, after the ferry docked a train journey to Victoria Station would follow. There, Helga's sister-in-law, Anni, accompanied by Victor, would be waiting for them.

Wulf and Helga had been invited over by Anni and Victor, and, using their cottage in Epping as a base, they planned to explore London. Apart from showing Wulf the usual tourist sights, Helga intended to take him to see one particular house in Putney – assuming it was still there, of course.

It was the house she had worked in as an au pair. Well, officially as an au pair. In reality her role had been as a companion for Mrs Castleford.

Mrs Castleford, Sitha…was she still living there? In her mind's eye Helga formed the image of the shy Indian girl. To help to adjust to the new ways, Sitha – and she, Helga, too – had attended English classes.

Would the one-time beauty still be good-looking now, Helga wondered. And what of Albert, what had become of him? He used to live next door and had befriended her.

Helga lifted up the next diary page but found that it had just one solitary sentence written right across it. Good Lord! She thought, looking at the shaky handwriting. Did I write this? *Just my rotten luck, gale force winds today!!!*

She considered the unfamiliar-looking, spidery letters. It seemed to her that the exclamation marks in particular resented being there. She chuckled to herself, envisaging them trying to somersault their way off the page.

Anyway, the short sentence had jolted her memory. Yes, it sure had been rough; definitely too rough to make notes, even if she had felt well enough...

But it was not until Helga read the ordinarily written page following on from the one with the spidery letters that she fully re-lived her earlier seafaring experience:

*I am writing this after arriving in Dover, while waiting for my train to London. I'm feeling better. Back on the ferry, I wanted to die. At one point I had to rush away from where I was sitting. Managed to squeeze past a hefty old lady and her equally rotund daughter, my shoulder bag kept getting entangled in their clothing. In my passable English I uttered an excuse. Swallowing hard, I said, "I've got to go. Sorry." The two women nodded sympathetically.*

*The boat was heaving and I picked my way along the topsy-turvy deck. I tried to avoid an empty beer can that was clattering towards me on the dull, wooden planks but its approach was too haphazard to be predicted and I stepped right onto it. Slipped, but managed with my free hand to hold on to the doorknob of the ladies' toilets. The knob turned under my weight and I was jerked inside, where, peering at me from the wall mirror I saw my ghostly reflection – the facial colour reminiscent of white sheets left too long unturned on a storage shelf. As I kept swallowing, blasts of cold air blew thankfully at me through the open windows up high and ruffled my long hair, very black against my deathly white skin.*

*But the raw gusts hid the pungent smell of sick only temporarily. Not wanting to put my bag down on the gluey floor I found a hook for it on the inside of the one remaining empty cubicle door. I had just enough time to lift up the lid…*

Helga gave a deep sigh. Glad it's calm today, she thought, and she let her gaze rest on the mirror-smooth sea. Looking sideways, she noted that Wulf was still absorbed in his magazine.

"In that case…" she murmured, and returned her attention back to her own reading matter.

It came to her as no surprise that the docking of the ferry had been no fun either. Apparently, within sight of Dover Harbour the people in her vicinity were overtaken by a wave of restlessness. The green deckchairs they had been sitting on got carelessly pushed aside to make more room at the windows. Other passengers deserted benches bolted to one side of the self-service restaurant and joined in to watch the ferry's progress.

Even before the boat came to a final halt the fretful or merely impatient streamed towards the luggage racks below. Keeping her distance, she had followed them down. But before long she found she was held captive within a mass of bodies on one of the stairways. Some young men fighting their way back up again lodged her more firmly amid the crowd. Protruding sharp corners of their backpacks got caught in fellow passengers' luggage, slowing the progress. Angry shouts and occasional squeals of pain could be heard above the shuffling of feet.

By way of an afterthought, so it seemed to Helga now, she had scribbled the remark: *This hassle and I could be sitting in the comfort of my own little room at home. What on earth possessed me to go on this journey to an uncertain future?*

Helga raised her head and stared into the distance. *But, she thought, I must have known the answer to that, surely. Probably I'd just felt sorry for myself when I jotted that question down. The quiet, studious me had finally had enough of Hannelore's taunts*: "Stay-at-home little sis is tied to Mother's apron strings. What a boring little fart she is!" *It had become a matter of pride for me to show Hannelore what I was made of, and go one better. Not only would I travel abroad, I would work there for a year and then go to university.*

Everybody admired Hannelore's sense of enterprise. Having pooh-poohed studying, she had joined the staff of the biggest Cologne travel bureau, been promoted to manageress, and as a top executive she regularly visited Australia and the Far East.

Unlike her sister, Helga was a home bird and did not like travelling. The tiresome preparations that went with it she found even less to her taste. There were dates to be agreed, tickets to be got, and then there was all the packing; not to mention the worry of something not going according to plan. Though, she was prepared to admit that the experience would not be half as bad if she could spirit herself to destinations.

As Helga turned the next page of her diary, she came across another heading in capital letters: FIRST IMPRESSIONS.

First impressions, but of what? Intrigued, she flicked ahead. She noticed sections with dialogue and remembered that at the time she had tried her hand at fiction, secretly hoping to emulate Hans Fallada. Would she now be embarrassed by her efforts?

FIRST IMPRESSIONS was spread over a thick wad of

pages. She counted ten of them before giving up. When had she written all of this? She would definitely not have had enough time to do it while she waited for her London train.

Besides, the appearance of the immaculate writing – with no crossings out and in the same green ink throughout – suggested to her that the entry had been copied at leisure, probably from a collection of shorter notes, and that she might have done so in one sitting.

In order to find an indication as to when the entry had been made, she scanned the text. It soon became clear to her that she had to have written the lengthy chapter at the end of her first week in England; at any rate, before Sitha Castleford's arrival in Putney.

Helga leaned back and made herself comfortable. Next to her, Wulf had been overcome by sleep. The computer magazine on his lap, he made contented chewing noises. Smiling indulgently, she thought that in the realms of dreamland he might be enjoying a favourite fruit tart. She lifted the text to her eyes.

*I asked the young man opposite me, "Are we going to London?" I wondered if I was on the right train, see. It had been speeding through the dark, chilly night for well over an hour without making a single stop at the stations we passed, and with mounting unease I had noticed the lights of yet another one whiz by.*

*"Yes," he replied, "to Victoria Station."*

*"Victoria Station?" I said, alarmed. "This train is not going to London?"*

*"Victoria Station is in London," he said with a smile. "We will soon be there. Where are you from?" he asked, putting his book to one side.*

*"From Germany."*

*"Bist du auf Urlaub in England?" he wanted to know.*

"*Du!!*" *he'd said. How dare he!*

*Coolly, and with finality in my voice, I replied, "No, not on holiday. Work." Then I leaned back and shut my eyes.*

Oh, dear, thought Helga. Shock and horror! *I'd had a lot to learn. He had used the familiar 'du' to address me and I'd immediately clammed up, taken aback by what seemed to me a clear-cut case of unseemly forwardness.*

Other things were not as they should have been. Contrary to what I had learned about the English from my school textbooks, I could not help noticing that strangers were talking to each other, and not just about the weather, and that without having first been introduced. And where were all those bowler-hatted, newspaper-reading gentlemen?

Eventually, the train was approaching a sea of lights. It had to be London. From below my seat I felt several short judders, in quick succession, followed each time by metallic churning within the undercarriage and resulting in the train's steady deceleration. Rows of terraced houses came into view, their small rectangular gardens pressed right against the steel netting of the railway perimeter. Through uncurtained windows shadowy beings could briefly be glimpsed.

"We'll be arriving at Victoria Station shortly," said the young man from across the row as I craned my neck trying to read the illuminated lettering on a high rise building. He nodded to me, pulled his briefcase from the luggage rack above his seat before making his way to the end of the wagon where the passengers had stored their heavy suitcases and bags.

The train pulled smoothly into the station. Doors were flung open and, breathing the cold damp night air, I heard the unfamiliar clank of porters' wheelbarrows. The station clock showed twenty past eleven. I should have arrived two hours ago.

The suitcases weighed me down, and with the heavier of my two bags hanging from my neck – with every step it was swinging to and fro in front of me – I slowly followed the other passengers to the platform exit. Had to pause repeatedly. More delay.

Icy puffs of wind swirled up discarded newspaper pages and crumpled brown paper bags, several crushed match boxes came sliding along the paving stones.

Near the line of taxis I set my cases down once more. I took a folded piece of paper from my coat pocket, briefly glanced at the address written on it and approached one of the black vehicles with the 'For Hire' sign lit up. Even though I had not seen a real life London taxi before, it looked oddly familiar, just like its picture postcard image.

Once inside the cab, I worried about being late. What if the Castlefords are angry with me turning up at such a late hour? Would they open the door?

Along the brightly-lit Millbank there was still continuous traffic. I recognised the palatial Tate Gallery building, Big Ben came into view soon after. (Soon after? Or was it before? Not so sure now.) Anyway, the clock chimed twelve times as the taxi passed the Houses of Parliament. Fifteen minutes on the driver stopped.

I was in a residential street, facing a high black iron fence. Behind it, in the taxi's headlights, I could make out an ivy-covered two-storey red brick house. It was well set back from the road. "That will be ten bob, for the tourist route," said the driver; he blinked as he turned his head towards me. Bob? I knew about pounds, shillings, pence, of guineas. But bob? I handed him a five pound note and was relieved when he returned the change.

I pushed the heavy gate open. There were no lights on inside the house. Behind me, the taxi pulled away. All was quiet. Too quiet. What if nobody answers the door? I should have asked the driver to wait until someone opened up. If I got no reply, I could have gone back to the station, stayed there until tomorrow morning. Wouldn't want to spend the night out here.

I shivered as I climbed the four stone steps to the entrance porch. My heart was beating fast. Put my suitcases down and looked for a name-plate. There was none. All I could see was a gleaming brass bell button. When I, tentatively, pressed down on it the loud buzz it emitted startled me. I waited.

Everything remained quiet inside. I was just about to press the button again when there was a flash of light from the glazed top of the mahogany entrance door. I heard a shuffling of feet, then the heavy door was partly pulled open.

"So...yes?" asked a thin voice.

In front of me stood a tiny, elderly man. Chinese? He looked emaciated. Strands of wispy white hair hung loosely to below his ears. Underneath the much-too-large maroon dressing gown he was clad in cream-coloured shiny pyjamas. As he stepped forward the gown's belt cord started to untie and both ends of it swung from his hips, pendulum-like, almost touching the delicate embroidered silk slippers.

"Oh...hm," I blundered, "I mean, is Mrs Castleford there?"

"You Miss Hoffnung?"

"Yes, that's right," I said relieved.

"Mr Castleford away on business. He back on weekend. Come, I show your room. I Mr Wu."

"I am sorry I am so late," I started on my prepared little speech. "The boat arrived two hours late in Dover and I had to wait for the last train." I felt guilty; I had obviously got Mr Wu out of bed.

"No matter," came the short but not unfriendly reply.

"Is Mrs Castleford not here?" I asked as I followed tiny but agile Mr Wu up the staircase. I was carrying one of my suitcases, had left the second, heavier one, in the hall.

"Mrs Castleford come from India next week," he said, turning sharply upon reaching the top of the landing. "Your room there." He pointed to the left. "Your room," he repeated on reaching the end of the landing and he pushed the door open.

"The children are with Mrs Castleford?"

"Children?" He sounded surprised. "No children, no." He shook his head. He turned to go, then stopped. "Tomorrow Mrs Widegate come. You speak Mrs Widegate. Yes, Mrs Widegate tomorrow morning, nine o'clock." He did not wait for a reply. "Good night," he called out politely before disappearing into a room across the entrance hall.

No children...I did not understand... . But Mr Wu knew my name, so I had to be in the right place.

I was more than happy with the room. Fawn-coloured wall to wall carpeting, supplemented by two large, deep-pile Indian rugs; I took my boots off and my feet sank into the soft fibres. The furniture was a blend of old and new, tastefully assembled. The room felt cosy and warm. There was a brand-new radiator under the windowsill.

It had been a long day and the warmth made me feel dopey. I looked at my suitcases on the floor, still unpacked, and yawned. Anyway, I unpacked the more delicate dresses and blouses and arranged these on hangers in the wardrobe. Left the rest for the next day.

I was ready for bed. When I took the covers off the sofa bed I noticed an envelope with my name on it. Opened it and two ten pound notes slid out. There was nothing else in the envelope. Maybe Mrs Widegate would know about it? In the meantime I put the money back into the envelope and stuck it into an empty drawer of the Edwardian writing desk.

Mrs Widegate was humming the popular Cliff Richard song 'Livin' Doll' as I walked into the downstairs kitchen.

"Good morning," I said.

Mrs Widegate who stood bent over the kitchen sink doing the washing-up half turned her head. She gave a brief smile and then continued with the dishes. Her shirtsleeves were pushed up well above the elbows, exposing her muscular arms. Presently, she pulled out the plug from the sink, and while the water gurgled away she dried her hands. Still holding the towel in front of her, the short matronly figure advanced towards me. I had stayed at the kitchen door.

"Morning," said Mrs Widegate and sort of inspected me. Because I was much taller she had to look up at me. "Do you want some breakfast?" she asked.

"Yes, please," I said.

Mrs Widegate busied herself with the kettle before placing two heavy beakers onto the shiny wooden table. She then rummaged about in the larder and produced a large packet of cornflakes. "Will a boiled egg be all right?" she asked, holding the fridge door ajar.

"Yes, please," I said again.

"Come and sit down," urged Mrs Widegate, as I was still standing at the entrance door.

"What shall I call you?"

"I am Helga Hoffnung. The new au pair."

"Yes, I know," said Mrs Widegate impatiently. "Shall I call you Helga or Miss Hoffnung?"

"Oh, sorry. Helga."

"All right...and I am Mary to you."

A sudden warm smile crossed Mrs Widegate's face and encouraged me.

"Mr Wu said last night that there are no children. I thought...I mean, what will I be doing here?"

"Children! I should think not! Mr and Mrs Castleford haven't been married long enough. Mrs Castleford is coming back from India next Thursday, yes, a week from today. As for your work,

I've no idea I'm sure. But I expect Mr Castleford will talk to you about that on Saturday."

Mary suddenly patted her forehead. "That reminds me, I am to tell you to go out and about, see the sights." And brushing my folded hands, she added, "He's left an envelope in your room with some spending money. Also, before I forget, I'd better give you these," and she pushed a set of keys across the table.

I was still digesting the various pieces of information while Mary extolled Mr Castleford's generous nature: "I've been working as a housekeeper for many years, but none of my previous employers come up to scratch. You'll like working here. Mr Castleford is a real gentleman."

Pouring out the tea, Mary talked on. "I come in to work three days a week. Every Thursday to Saturday, nine to twelve. I look after the house, do the laundry and get the weekend shopping. Mr Wu usually writes out the list for me. I used to work for the Johnsons before and when Mr Castleford bought the house nine months ago he kept me on. He's got another flat in Putney where he's been staying most of the time. Haven't met his wife, though that's about to happen." Mary knitted her brow. "He did say things wouldn't change...I suppose I'll have to wait and see."

From the back of the house came the sound of heavy footsteps. When I heard what seemed to be a scraping of boots against metal I looked up. It was coming from outside the kitchen.

"That will be Joseph," Mary said. "He's been working here for ever so many years. Now it's getting cold he comes in every day to see to the coal burner down in the cellar, does odd jobs and tends the garden when it needs doing. He's a grumpy old dear, doesn't say much."

As he clunked into the kitchen, Mary said, "Want a cuppa?"

"Yap," he said, tapping with his index finger against the peak of his dark-blue cap. He rubbed his large, leathery hands, trying to warm them and make them pliable. Still, his fingers only just obeyed him in the unbuttoning of his duffle coat.

It must have seen better days, I thought, watching him drop the frayed and roughly mended coat to the floor next to where he sat down. He cleared his throat repeatedly, pulled out a large check cotton handkerchief, unfolded it ceremoniously, shook it, then blew his nose. The cloth vibrated in the process.

"And who would you be?" he asked in a surly manner, clicking his teeth, looking sideways at me, the stranger.

"That's Helga. Remember I told you – "

"And where would she be from?" Joseph cut in brusquely.

"From Germany." This time I answered for myself.

Joseph sat up very erect. "Germany! Hey!"

The hostility in his voice made me sit up too.

"Right," he snapped, "I'm off." He leaped to his feet, losing his balance momentarily; he knocked against the table and upset the tea mugs. I caught a glance of his flushed face as he picked up his drink before storming to the back door.

Once there, he turned around, and, addressing Mary Widegate, he hissed: "What with him" – Joseph moved his head in the direction of Mr Wu's room – "and now, now her! Now we've really hit the jackpot!" He slammed the door behind him.

"Silly man! Don't you take any notice of him." The anger in Mary's voice changed to sympathy. "You didn't make him a prisoner of war. Silly man," she repeated, shaking her head.

I didn't know what to say, just sat there, white-faced, shamed. When I felt tears welling up inside I rushed out of the kitchen, yearning for the privacy of my room. I narrowly missed colliding with Mr Wu, who, fastidiously dressed and carrying a fine bone china cup and saucer on a black lacquer tray, let out a loud shriek.

"I'm off," called Mary after a while from below the stairs. "Help yourself to the food. There's plenty in the fridge, and in the larder. Cheerio."

Before I had time to ask how to work the hyper-modern cooker, Mary had pulled the front door shut; her short precise steps carried her speedily away, towards the gates.

The sun was trying to break through the hazy mist. At best, it managed a pale watery sheen. The November air tasted raw.

Well, when I had first stepped outside, that first afternoon, a stranger in a strange land, I did not think it was all that cold. But after wandering about for an hour or so I could feel the damp air's invading grip. (Yet, the puddles in the road were not even frozen. An above zero Celsius temperature would not have made me feel that cold back home.)

Being out in the capital city for the first time I looked into each and every display window on the busy and noisy high street. But where were the assorted cakes, pastries, tarts, the manifold variety of gateaux, the chocolate titbits, marzipan fruits? All of these I had expected to find in a London cake shop. Similarly, at a butcher's I missed the array of cold meats and sausages, salamis hanging from hooks. Black pudding and cooked ham was all there was. Then, to my consternation, I noticed that some of the cuts of meat had prominent labels stuck onto them: BUY THE BEST, BUY BRITISH. I shook my head. I could not remember having seen a comparable label back home. BUY THE BEST, BUY GERMAN? No way. Would it even be allowed? – might be interpreted as overtly nationalistic?

An appetite-inducing tang wafted across the road. Following my nose, I soon found its source: a Wimpy Bar. Sampling the 'Today's Special' at my window seat, I overlooked a busy bus stop only meters away. Was impressed by the orderly queuing. The bus arrived and there was no mad scramble to get on, no pushing, shoving, elbowing. How civilized it all was.

Yet, the next moment, a well-dressed elderly lady had no

compunction in dropping her bonbon wrapper onto the pavement. And that in full view of a bobby!

※

After lunch on Saturday I set out for Westminster. Stopped off in a small park that was used as a short cut to the underground station, sat down on one of its deserted benches and opened my newly acquired London A – Z.

Just as I stood up from my seat, I froze. My legs gave way and I was back on the bench, one arm gripping the side of it. The map I had been about to stuff into my bag flopped to the ground. Right in front of me, watching me, sat a big black furry beast – or so I thought.

I was not used to dogs, always felt uneasy passing one of their kind in the street. I remembered hearing that one must not show fear, and not to stare – not easy when you are petrified.

"Where's your master?" I eventually mumbled, stiffly leaning forward. But the hoped-for whistle or call of the owner did not come. Instead, the dog, bum on ground, shuffled closer. He started to sniff up and down my trouser legs. Soft fur was brushing against my left hand. I did not dare move. "Good dog," I said, trying to convince myself of the animal's peaceful intentions. Then I felt my feet pinned down by the dog's weight as he stretched out in front of me.

You're not in any hurry, I thought, looking down on the heap of fur warming my ankles. Maybe, if I move my feet out slowly...

Managed to free myself, picked up my things and made a few cautious steps away from the bench. I turned my head. The dog was following me. There was still no sign of any owner.

"You'd better go home," I said. Somehow encouraged, he wagged his tail and bounced to my side, keeping pace.

Less fearful now, I dared to give my companion a quick pat on his head, and he rewarded me with antics of tail-chasing.

*I stopped near the park exit, from there I could see the entrance to the tube beckoning. "Look, you'll have to go home," I told the dog.*

*What am I going to do with you, I asked myself as I stood bent down, stroking the animal's head? The dog looked at me, eyes full of trust. With his ears tilted he appeared to listen earnestly. "Maybe if we wait a little longer your boss will turn up?"*

*The two of us walked back into the park and I sat down on another bench. My charge jumped up next to me and without further ado he laid his head on my lap.*

*Twenty minutes later we were still occupying that bench; though, in the meantime, my furry friend had polished off the lion's share of my packet of Morning Coffee.*

*When I rubbed my face into his soft furry neck I felt something hard. Buried deep within his coat I discovered a small round metal disk. Pulled it to the surface, imprinted on it was an address.*

*"I suppose I'd better take you home," I said. "You've got yourself lost, haven't you?" He responded by lifting his head and raising his floppy velvety ears.*

※

Helga stopped reading her diary. She put the loose page she had been holding down on the table in front of her. With the dog's picture clearly in her mind, she remembered how he had led her to Albert, who, though she did not know it then, would become a good friend.

Circle Road ran parallel to Parkside Avenue – the leafy avenue the Castlefords resided in. At number forty-one Circle Road, which was situated at the back of the Castlefords, Helga caught up with the dog. Having raced ahead, he was frantically jumping up at the gate and barking most excitedly. As soon as she released the latch, he tore along the path to the rear of the building, disappearing from sight. She was just in time to see the door to the ground-floor flat being opened...

She had witnessed the dog's reunion with his master. The predominantly black animal – the patches of white under his belly were usually hidden from view – was standing on his hind legs, eye to eye with a skinny figure in a wheelchair. Pinned to the back of his chair, his face, neck, any bare area of skin was being savoured by the dog's lapping tongue. After a moment or two, she heard the man's firm voice: "What have you done? Bad boy. Get down!" he ordered. The dog responded at once. Tail between legs, head held low, ears droopy, he slunk off.

Albert introduced himself and invited her in. With leather-gloved hands, he rolled his chair backwards to make more room for her to enter. "Thank you for bringing Jester back," he said, even before he had offered her the one easy chair in the living room. "Watch out for the spiky spring," he warned. When she pressed down on the seat before lowering herself onto it, he laughed. He had a sparkle in his eyes and seemed utterly relaxed so that her initial discomfiture of meeting with a disabled person evaporated.

As time wore on and they talked, his appearance lost its strangeness. She no longer noticed the thinness of his body, his sticklike arms, the withered legs. What was more, she had the feeling that he knew what his effect on her had been and he made her not mind her thoughts.

During their first meeting Albert told Helga several times how relieved he was that she had brought Jester back to him. "Twice that dog has now absconded. My friend, Jim, found him last time. He's still out looking for him. Where exactly in the park did you find Jester?"

"I didn't, he found me," Helga said. "He came up to me and just wouldn't leave me." And as if in confirmation,

Jester trotted across the living room and lay down at her feet. "To think that I was frightened of you." She reached for Jester's paw and stroked it. "Especially as we're practically neighbours."

"Okay, come here," Albert said, aware that Jester was shooting him doleful glances. "You're forgiven," and he patted him on the head.

Delighted, Jester bounced into the middle of the room, turned himself into a heap of black and white fluff with jabbing sticky legs thrashing the air.

❦

Helga and Wulf walked out of the house, which a long time ago had belonged to the Castlefords. The outside of it had hardly changed, while the inside was unrecognisable.

The once imposing residence had been turned into a Centre For Transcendental Meditation. What had been the entrance hall now functioned as the reception area. As she approached the smart desk with the smiling well-groomed receptionist, it occurred to Helga that the desk stood in Mr Wu's former bedroom.

Though disappointed that Helga and Wulf were not enrolling as new clients of the Centre, the oriental lady listened with interest to Helga's query.

Meena, that was her name, could not help, but she called the youngish handyman who had been at the Centre the longest, right from the time it opened, fifteen years ago. He knew that the house had belonged to a 'city gent', but Castleford had definitely not been his name.

"Maybe we'll have better luck with Albert," said Helga as she led the way to his former flat. The building, which had housed it also looked much the same, except that the pathway to the ground-floor rear entrance now led along manicured lawns where once deep grass had sprouted.

A dark-suited man in his thirties opened the door. "Albert? No, sorry, I don't know anyone of that name," he said apologetically, shaking his head.

"Not to worry." Helga gave him a smile. "As I said, forty years is a long time." She turned to go but remarked, "His wheelchair ramp is still here, so there's something that he left behind."

"Wait a moment," the man called out, stepping onto the top of the ramp. "Boy Bridges did live here until five years ago. He was an electric wheelchair user and known as a bit of an eccentric – kept changing his name. Maybe it was Albert when you knew him? Apparently he always wore a black Stetson. Maybe he did then?"

The man did not wait for an answer. As he spoke he had become increasingly animated. "Anyway," he continued, and there was veneration in his voice, "He now calls himself Eric Mahler; it's the name he paints under. I own one of his paintings."

He looked from Helga to Wulf and back to Helga. "I've got an idea," he said; "Eric Mahler's photograph is on several of his exhibition previews. Why don't you come in and check it out?"

While the man, Daniel Elliot as they had learned, went to fetch the brochures, Helga remembered Albert's living room. The room she and Wulf were now sitting in bore little resemblance to it. In place of Albert's few pieces of furniture, which had been glaringly at odds with each other, she noted the matching suite and elegant bookcase. The writing desk near the window was fashioned of dark wood, with its lustrous surface and the embellishments it oozed quality. Where there had been frayed carpet cut-offs in a hideous bright red, expensive runners now covered the wall-to-wall carpeting.

At the time, matching items of furniture had been an unaffordable luxury for Albert; it was the last thing on his mind. Serviceability was the prime objective while he struggled to live independently. Though he had owned a first-class guitar on which he performed in gigs and entertained at home.

When Daniel Elliot returned with a pile of catalogues and brochures showing Eric Mahler's paintings and, in three cases, his photograph, Helga confirmed that the artist was indeed Albert. His once black hair and beard were now grey, but the features were unmistakably his.

Bombarded with questions, Daniel told his visitors all he knew: he had bumped into the artist during the exchange of keys. Noticing Daniel's interest in his folder full of sketches, which needed to be collected from the flat, Boy Bridges, as he was then, promised to send an invite to his forthcoming exhibition. It had been a local one. Daniel had fallen in love with the work, and from then on he attended every preview, even if it meant travelling long distances away from London. Apparently, years ago, in his search for peace and solitude, the artist had discovered Lincolnshire, and in particular the area around Boston. On one of his travels he had come across a gallery there, in Swineshead, which had offered to keep some of his work permanently on show. Daniel had visited there.

"I'm about to go again, to see the current mixed exhibition with some of Eric Mahler's work," Daniel said, and presented Helga with the respective illustrated catalogue. "You keep it. I'll pick up another copy. Who knows?" He added, "The people in the gallery might give you his address. I believe, around the time he left here, he bought an adapted mobile home, next to a farm, somewhere out there in the sticks."

❧

Later, in the evening, Helga was still excited when she told Anni and Victor about meeting Daniel Elliot and finding out about Albert. As soon as she mentioned his alter ego, Eric Mahler, Victor got up from his seat.

"Come with me," he said, and he led Helga, followed by the others, to the painting on his study wall. "See that!" He pointed to the signature on *Beginnings*. "I had no idea that you knew the artist."

"Well," said Helga, "he wasn't a painter when I knew him. He was a musician then, played the guitar. He must've taken up painting later. It's definitely him," she assured Victor, seeing the way he had started to screw up his face and scratched behind his ear.

"You know," Victor said, "for years I'd wanted to show Anni the gallery where I found *Beginnings*. Never got round to it." He shook his head in amazement: "Unbelievable, just unbelievable," he repeated.

Back in the living room, he asked to see the catalogue Helga had been given. "I see," he said, bending over the table and looking at the Eric Mahler section, "he produces traditional paintings as well. I like that landscape." He pointed to the *Big Sky*. "That figures, yes, the big skies over the Lincolnshire Fens. I remember. And what powerful seascapes! Now, they remind me of *Beginnings*."

He picked up the catalogue and carried it to his chair. While the others talked amongst themselves, he looked at the rest of the illustrations.

It took no time at all for Victor to make up his mind. Back at the table he rapped it hard with his knuckles. "I suggest we all take a trip to Swineshead. Tomorrow. What do you say? Is it a date?"

Acknowledging the general murmur of approval, he could not refrain himself. "Bloody good work all round," he said, "that gallery has paintings by Andrzej Kuhn, Malcolm Doughty, Eric Mahler and John Grove. It's magic. And nobody has heard of the place!"

# *Acclaim for* Silent Shadows

Eva Maria Ghoshal, who writes under her maiden name, Knabenbauer, won the fiction category with *Silent Shadows*, the 'gripping and moving' story of a young woman returning to East Germany, from which she escaped …"

*Writers' News*

This year's First Prize for excellence and accomplishment was awarded by The David St John Thomas Charitable Trust: "Eva Maria Knabenbauer draws her central character skilfully, and we find ourselves identifying with this woman who goes on a journey into her past…and its (Silent Shadows) flashbacks to life under Russian occupation are particularly fascinating…"

*Judges of The David St John Thomas Charitable Trust,*
*2003 Fiction Award*

"*Silent Shadows* tells what some of them (escapees from the former GDR trying to reconnect with relatives, friends and acquaintances) found within the confines of the small town of Aschersleben. This is touchingly set out in this book with a love story woven in. It is a small volume which should really be read by anyone trying to understand how the DDR (GDR) worked out, how it enmeshed its population in a Russian-controlled society… . This is such an interesting and topical book that we hope, space permitting, to publish with the author's permission some typical excerpts from it in the July issue of the REVIEW."

*British-German Review*

"In Eva Maria Knabenbauer's new book, *Silent Shadows*, the year is 1991, the Wall is down and an apprehensive Anni, now living in England, returns to the East German town she fled as a young woman of twenty in the last months before the barrier was built… . As Anni progresses on her journey, there are frequent flashbacks to earlier days – memories of her father, memories of her mother, the day when the Russian troops arrived… . Her journey into days long gone is set against her growing relationship with Victor, a passion which itself is affected by a love affair from the past. At the end it seems that, although the physical barrier of the Wall is gone, a new, invisible one may have risen in its place…

"Unlike many authors, Knabenbauer has first-hand knowledge of the whisperings and the suspicions, the fears and the hopes of those caught up in the crazy days before the Wall was built, because she was there. This unusual book is essentially a love story with a powerful message that there is no going back and that the past is, indeed, a country we cannot visit – with or without a Wall to keep us out."

*Lincolnshire Echo*

"You can't go home again. But Anni does, to confront all the fears of early life in the hateful repression of Communist East Germany. This is more than a sentimental journey. Ghosts from her past reappear and bitter sweet memories surface like old scars. The overall effect is cathartic and facing up to her former life allows Anni to abandon her reservations and embrace her new life in the West. At its heart Eva Maria Knabenbauer's novel *Silent Shadows* is a touching and compelling story about love."

*Sir Trevor McDonald, OBE*